The Chase of the Golden Plate

The Chase of the Golden Plate

Jacques Futrelle

Published by Hesperus Press Limited
28 Mortimer Street, London W1W 7RD
www.hesperuspress.com

First published in 1906
First published by Hesperus Press Limited, 2012

Designed and typeset by Fraser Muggeridge studio
Printed in Jordan by Jordan National Press

ISBN: 978-1-84391-360-3

CONTENTS

Part 1:
The Burglar and the Girl

CHAPTER 1

Cardinal Richelieu and the Mikado stepped out on a narrow balcony overlooking the entrance to Seven Oaks, lighted their cigarettes and stood idly watching the throng as it poured up the wide marble steps. Here was an over-corpulent Dowager Empress of China, there an Indian warrior in full paint and toggery, and mincing along behind him two giggling Geisha girls. Next, in splendid robes of rank, came the Czar of Russia. The Mikado smiled.

'An old enemy of mine,' he remarked to the Cardinal.

A Watteau Shepherdess was assisted out of an automobile by Christopher Columbus and they came up the walk arm-in-arm, while a Pierrette ran beside them laughing up into their faces. D'Artagnan, Athos, Aramis, and Porthos swaggered along with insolent, clanking swords.

'Ah!' exclaimed the Cardinal. 'There are four gentlemen whom I know well.'

Mary Queen of Scots, Pocahontas, the Sultan of Turkey, and Mr Micawber chatted amicably together in one language. Behind them came a figure which immediately arrested attention. It was a Burglar, with dark lantern in one hand and revolver in the other. A black mask was drawn down to his lips, a slouch hat shaded his eyes, and a kit of the tools of his profession swung from one shoulder.

'By George!' commented the Cardinal. 'Now, that's clever.'

'Looks like the real thing,' the Mikado added.

The Burglar stood aside a moment, allowing a diamond-burdened Queen Elizabeth to pass, then came on up the steps. The Cardinal and the Mikado passed through an open window into the reception-room to witness his arrival.

'Her Royal Highness, Queen Elizabeth!' the graven-faced servant announced.

The Burglar handed a card to the liveried Voice and noted, with obvious amusement, a fleeting expression of astonishment on the stolid face. Perhaps it was there because the card had been offered in that hand which held the revolver. The Voice glanced at the name on the card and took a deep breath of relief.

'Bill, the Burglar!' he announced.

There was a murmur of astonishment and interest in the reception-hall and the ballroom beyond. Thus it was that the Burglar found himself the centre of attention for a moment, while a ripple of laughter ran around. The entrance of a Clown, bounding in behind him, drew all eyes away, however, and the Burglar was absorbed in the crowd.

It was only a few minutes later that Cardinal Richelieu and the Mikado, seeking diversion, isolated the Burglar and dragged him off to the smoking room. There the Czar of Russia, who was on such terms of intimacy with the Mikado that he called him Mike, joined them and they smoked together.

'How did you ever come to hit on a costume like that?' asked the Cardinal of the Burglar.

The Burglar laughed, disclosing two rows of strong, white teeth. A cleft in the square-cut, clean-shaven chin, visible below the mask, became more pronounced. A woman would have called it a dimple.

'I wanted something different,' he explained. 'I couldn't imagine anything more extraordinary than a real burglar here ready to do business, so I came.'

'It's lucky the police didn't see you,' remarked the Czar.

Again the Burglar laughed. He was evidently a good-natured craftsman, despite his sinister garb.

'That was my one fear – that I would be pinched before I arrived,' he replied. '"Pinched", I may explain, is a technical term in my profession meaning jugged, nabbed, collared, run in. It seemed that my fears had some foundation, too, for when I drove up in my auto and stepped out a couple of plain-clothes men stared at me pretty hard.'

He laid aside the dark lantern and revolver to light a fresh cigarette. The Mikado picked up the lantern and flashed the light on and off several times, while the Czar sighted the revolver at the floor.

'Better not do that,' suggested the Burglar casually. 'It's loaded.'

'Loaded?' repeated the Czar. He laid down the revolver gingerly.

'Surest thing, you know,' and the Burglar laughed quizzically. 'I'm the real thing, you see, so naturally my revolver is loaded. I think I ought to be able to make quite a good haul, as we say, before unmasking-time.'

'If you're as clever as your appearance would indicate,' said the Cardinal admiringly, 'I see no reason why it shouldn't be worthwhile. You might, for instance, make a collection of Elizabethan jewels. I have noticed four Elizabeths so far, and it's early yet.'

'Oh, I'll make it pay,' the Burglar assured him lightly. 'I'm pretty clever; practised a good deal, you know. Just to show you that I am an expert, here is a watch and pin I took from my friend, the Czar, five minutes ago.'

He extended a well-gloved hand in which lay the watch and diamond pin. The Czar stared at them a moment in frank astonishment; patted himself all over in sudden trepidation; then laughed sheepishly. The Mikado tilted his cigar up to a level with the slant eyes of his mask, and laughed.

'In the language of diplomacy, Nick,' he told the Czar, 'you are what is known as "easy". I thought I had convinced you of that.'

'Gad, you are clever,' remarked the Cardinal. 'I might have used you along with D'Artagnan and the others.'

The Burglar laughed again and stood up lazily.

'Come on, this is stupid,' he suggested. 'Let's go out and see what's doing.'

'Say, just between ourselves tell us who you are,' urged the Czar. 'Your voice seems familiar, but I can't place you.'

'Wait till unmasking-time,' retorted the Burglar good-naturedly. 'Then you'll know. Or if you think you could bribe that stone image who took my card at the door you might try. He'll remember me. I never saw a man so startled in all my life as he was when I appeared.'

The quartet sauntered out into the ballroom just as the signal for the grand march was given. A few minutes later the kaleidoscopic picture began to move. Stuyvesant Randolph, the host, as Sir Walter Raleigh, and his superb wife, as Cleopatra, looked upon the mass of colour, and gleaming shoulders, and jewels, and brilliant uniforms, and found it good – extremely good.

Mr Randolph smiled behind his mask at the striking incongruities on every hand: Queen Elizabeth and Mr Micawber; Cardinal Richelieu and a Pierrette; a Clown dancing attendance on Marie Antoinette. The Czar of Russia paid deep and devoted attention to a light-footed Geisha girl, while the Mikado and Folly, a jingling thing in bells and abbreviated skirts, romped together.

The grotesque figure of the march was the Burglar. His revolver was thrust carelessly into a pocket and the dark lantern hung at his belt. He was pouring a stream of pleasing nonsense into the august ear of Lady Macbeth, nimbly seeking at the same time to evade the pompous train of the Dowager Empress. The grand march came to an end and the chattering throng broke up into little groups.

Cardinal Richelieu strolled along with a Pierrette on his arm.

'Business good?' he inquired of the Burglar.

'Expect it to be,' was the reply.

The Pierrette came and, standing on her tip-toes – silly, impractical sort of toes they were – made a *moue* at the Burglar.

'Oooh!' she exclaimed. 'You are perfectly horrid.'

'Thank you,' retorted the Burglar.

He bowed gravely, and the Cardinal, with his companion, passed on. The Burglar stood gazing after them a moment, then glanced around the room, curiously, two or three times. He might have been looking for someone. Finally he wandered away aimlessly through the crowd.

CHAPTER 2

Half an hour later the Burglar stood alone, thoughtfully watching the dancers as they whirled by. A light hand fell on his arm – he started a little – and in his ear sounded a voice soft with the tone of a caress.

'Excellent, Dick, excellent!'

The Burglar turned quickly to face a girl – a Girl of the Golden West, with deliciously rounded chin, slightly parted rose-red lips, and sparkling, eager eyes as blue as – as blue as – well, they were blue eyes. An envious mask hid cheeks and brow, but above, a sombrero was perched arrogantly on crisp, ruddy-gold hair, flaunting a tricoloured ribbon. A revolver swung at her hip – the wrong hip – and a Bowie knife, singularly inoffensive in appearance, was thrust through her girdle. The Burglar looked curiously a moment, then smiled.

'How did you know me?' he asked.

'By your chin,' she replied. 'You can never hide yourself behind a mask that doesn't cover that.'

The Burglar touched his chin with one gloved hand.

'I forgot that,' he remarked ruefully.

'Hadn't you seen me?'

'No.'

The Girl drew nearer and laid one hand lightly on his arm; her voice dropped mysteriously.

'Is everything ready?' she asked.

'Oh, yes,' he assured her quickly. His voice, too, was lowered cautiously.

'Did you come in the auto?'

'Yes.'

'And the casket?'

For an instant the Burglar hesitated.

'The casket?' he repeated.

'Certainly, the casket. Did you get it all right?'

The Burglar looked at her with a new, business-like expression on his lips. The Girl returned his steady gaze for an instant, then her eyes dropped. A faint colour glowed in her white chin. The Burglar suddenly laughed admiringly.

'Yes, I got it,' he said.

She took a deep breath quickly, and her white hands fluttered a little.

'We will have to go in a few minutes, won't we?' she asked uneasily.

'I suppose so,' he replied.

'Certainly before unmasking-time,' she said, 'because – because I think there is someone here who knows, or suspects, that –'

'Suspects what?' demanded the Burglar.

'Sh-h-h-h!' warned the Girl, and she laid a finger on her lips. 'Not so loud. Someone might hear. Here are some people coming now that I'm afraid of. They know me. Meet me in the conservatory in five minutes. I don't want them to see me talking to you.'

She moved away quickly and the Burglar looked after her with admiration and some impalpable quality other than that in his eyes. He was turning away toward the conservatory when he ran into the arms of an oversized man lumpily clad in the dress of a courtier. The lumpy individual stood back and sized him up.

'Say, young fellow, that's a swell rig you got there,' he remarked.

The Burglar glanced at him in polite astonishment – perhaps it was the tone of the remark.

'Glad you like it,' he said coldly, and passed on.

As he waited in the conservatory the amusement died out of his eyes and his lips were drawn into a straight, sharp line. He had seen the lumpy individual speak to another man, indicating generally the direction of the conservatory as he did so. After a moment the Girl returned in deep agitation.

'We must go now – at once,' she whispered hurriedly. 'They suspect us. I know it, I know it!'

'I'm afraid so,' said the Burglar grimly. 'That's why that detective spoke to me.'

'Detective?' gasped the Girl.

'Yes, a detective disguised as a gentleman.'

'Oh, if they are watching us what shall we do?'

The Burglar glanced out, and seeing the man to whom the lumpy individual had spoken coming toward the conservatory, turned suddenly to the Girl.

'Do you really want to go with me?' he asked.

'Certainly,' she replied eagerly.

'You are making no mistake?'

'No, Dick, no!' she said again. 'But if we are caught –'

'Do as I say and we won't be caught,' declared the Burglar. His tone now was sharp, commanding. 'You go on alone toward the front door. Pass out as if to get a breath of fresh air. I'll follow in a minute. Watch for me. This detective is getting too curious for comfort. Outside we'll take the first auto and run for it.'

He thoughtfully whirled the barrel of his revolver in his fingers as he stared out into the ballroom. The Girl clung to him helplessly a moment; her hand trembled on his arm.

'I'm frightened,' she confessed. 'Oh, Dick, if –'

'Don't lose your nerve,' he commanded. 'If you do we'll both be caught. Go on now, and do as I say. I'll come – but I may come in a hurry. Watch for me.'

For just a moment more the Girl clung to his arm.

'Oh, Dick, you darling!' she whispered. Then, turning, she left him there.

From the door of the conservatory the Burglar watched her splendid, lithe figure as she threaded her way through the crowd. Finally she passed beyond his view and he sauntered carelessly toward the door. Once he glanced back. The lumpy individual was following slowly. Then he saw a liveried servant approach the host and whisper to him excitedly.

'This is my cue to move,' the Burglar told himself grimly.

Still watching, he saw the servant point directly at him. The host, with a sudden gesture, tore off his mask and the Burglar accelerated his pace.

'Stop that man!' called the host.

For one brief instant there was the dead silence which follows general astonishment – and the Burglar ran for the door. Several pairs of hands reached out from the crowd toward him.

'There he goes, there!' exclaimed the Burglar excitedly. 'That man ahead! I'll catch him!'

The ruse opened the way and he went through. The Girl was waiting at the foot of the steps.

'They're coming!' he panted as he dragged her along. 'Climb in that last car on the end there!'

Without a word the Girl ran to the auto and clambered into the front seat. Several men dashed out of the house. Wonderingly her eyes followed the vague figure of the Burglar as he sped along in the shadow of a wall. He paused beneath a window, picked up something and raced for the car.

'Stop him!' came a cry.

The Burglar flung his burden, which fell at the Girl's feet with a clatter, and leaped. The auto swayed as he landed beside her. With a quick twist of the wheel he headed out.

'Hurry, Dick, they're coming!' gasped the Girl.

The motor beneath them whirred and panted and the car began to move.

'Halt, or I'll fire,' came another cry.

'Down!' commanded the Burglar.

His hand fell on the Girl's shoulder heavily and he dragged her below the level of the seat. Then, bending low over the wheel, he gave the car half power. It leaped out into the road in the path of its own light, just as there came a pistol-shot from behind, followed instantly by another.

The car sped on.

CHAPTER 3

Stuyvesant Randolph, millionaire, owner of Seven Oaks and host of the masked ball, was able to tell the police only what happened, and not the manner of its happening. Briefly, this was that a thief, cunningly disguised as a Burglar with dark lantern and revolver in hand, had surreptitiously attended the masked ball by entering at the front door and presenting an invitation card. And when Mr Randolph got this far in his story even he couldn't keep his face straight.

The sum total of everyone's knowledge, therefore, was this: soon after the grand march a servant entered the smoking room and found the Burglar there alone, standing beside an open window, looking out. This smoking room connected, by a corridor, with a small dining room where the Randolph gold plate was kept in ostentatious seclusion. As the servant entered the smoking room the Burglar turned away from the window and went out into the ballroom. He did not carry a bundle; he did not appear to be excited.

Fifteen or twenty minutes later the servant discovered that eleven plates of the gold service, valued roughly at $15,000, were missing. He informed Mr Randolph. The information, naturally enough, did not elevate the host's enjoyment of the ball, and he did things hastily.

Meanwhile – that is, between the time when the Burglar left the smoking room and the time when he passed out the front door – the Burglar had talked earnestly with a masked Girl of the West. It was established that, when she left him in the conservatory, she went out the front door. There she was joined by the Burglar, and then came their sensational flight in the automobile – a forty horsepower car that moved like the wind. The automobile in which the

Burglar had gone to Seven Oaks was left behind; thus far it had not been claimed.

The identity of the Burglar and the Girl made the mystery. It was easy to conjecture – that's what the police said – how the Burglar got away with the gold plate. He went into the smoking room, then into the dining room, dropped the gold plate into a sack and threw the sack out of a window. It was beautifully simple. Just what the Girl had to do with it wasn't very clear; perhaps a score or more articles of jewelry, which had been reported missing by guests, engaged her attention.

It was also easy to see how the Burglar and the Girl had been able to shake off pursuit by the police in two other automobiles. The car they had chosen was admittedly the fastest of the scores there, the night was pitch-dark, and, besides, a Burglar like that was liable to do anything. Two shots had been fired at him by the lumpy courtier, who was really Detective Cunningham, but they had only spurred him on.

These things were easy to understand. But the identity of the pair was a different and more difficult proposition, and there remained the task of yanking them out of obscurity. This fell to the lot of Detective Mallory, who represented the Supreme Police Intelligence of the Metropolitan District, happily combining a No. 11 shoe and a No. 6 hat. He was a cautious, suspicious, far-seeing man – as police detectives go. For instance, it was he who explained the method of the theft with a lucidity that was astounding.

Detective Mallory and two or three of his satellites heard Mr Randolph's story, then the statements of his two men who had attended the ball in costume, and the statements of the servants. After all this Mr Mallory chewed his cigar and thought violently for several minutes. Mr Randolph looked on expectantly; he didn't want to miss anything.

'As I understand it, Mr Randolph,' said the Supreme Police Intelligence at last, 'each invitation-card presented at the door by your guests bore the name of the person to whom it was issued?'

'Yes,' replied Mr Randolph.

'Ah!' exclaimed the detective shrewdly. 'Then we have a clue.'

'Where are those cards, Curtis?' asked Mr Randolph of the servant who had received them at the door.

'I didn't know they were of further value, sir, and they were thrown away – into the furnace.'

Mr Mallory was crestfallen.

'Did you notice if the card presented at the door by the Burglar on the evening of the masked ball at Seven Oaks bore a name?' he asked. He liked to be explicit like that.

'Yes, sir. I noticed it particularly because the gentleman was dressed so queerly.'

'Do you remember the name?'

'No, sir.'

'Would you remember it if you saw it or heard it again?'

The servant looked at Mr Randolph helplessly.

'I don't think I would, sir,' he answered.

'And the Girl? Did you notice the card she gave you?'

'I don't remember her at all, sir. Many of the ladies wore wraps when they came in, and her costume would not have been noticeable if she had on a wrap.'

The Supreme Intelligence was thoughtful for another few minutes. At last he turned to Mr Randolph again.

'You are certain there was only one man at that ball dressed as a Burglar?' he asked.

'Yes, thank Heaven,' replied Mr Randolph fervently. 'If there'd been another one they might have taken the piano.'

The Supreme Intelligence frowned.

'And this girl was dressed like a Western girl?' he asked.

'Yes. A sort of Spirit-of-the-West costume.'

'And no other woman there wore such a dress?'

'No,' responded Mr Randolph.

'No,' echoed the two detectives.

'Now, Mr Randolph, how many invitations were issued for the ball?'

'Three or four hundred. It's a big house,' Mr Randolph apologised, 'and we tried to do the thing properly.'

'How many persons do you suppose actually attended the ball?'

'Oh, I don't know. Three hundred, perhaps.'

Detective Mallory thought again.

'It's unquestionably the work of two bold and clever professional crooks,' he said at last judicially, and his satellites hung on his words eagerly. 'It has every earmark of it. They perhaps planned the thing weeks before, and forged invitation-cards, or perhaps stole them – perhaps stole them.'

He turned suddenly and pointed an accusing finger at the servant, Curtis.

'Did you notice the handwriting on the card the Burglar gave you?' he demanded.

'No, sir. Not particularly.'

'I mean, do you recall if it was different in any way from the handwriting on the other cards?' insisted the Supreme Intelligence.

'I don't think it was, sir.'

'If it had been would you have noticed it?'

'I might have, sir.'

'Were the names written on all the invitation-cards by the same hand, Mr Randolph?'

'Yes: my wife's secretary.'

Detective Mallory arose and paced back and forth across the room with wrinkles in his brow.

'Ah!' he said at last, 'then we know the cards were not forged, but stolen from someone to whom they had been sent. We know this much, therefore –' he paused a moment.

'Therefore all that must be done,' Mr Randolph finished the sentence, 'is to find from whom the card or cards were stolen, who presented them at my door, and who got away with the plate.'

The Supreme Intelligence glared at him aggressively. Mr Randolph's face was perfectly serious. It was his gold plate, you know.

'Yes, that's it,' Detective Mallory assented. 'Now we'll get after this thing right. Downey, you get that automobile the Burglar left at Seven Oaks and find its owner; also find the car the Burglar and the Girl escaped in. Cunningham, you go to Seven Oaks and look over the premises. See particularly if the Girl left a wrap – she didn't wear one away from there – and follow that up. Blanton, you take a list of invited guests that Mr Randolph will give you, check off those persons who are known to have been at the ball, and find out all about those who were not, and – follow that up.'

'That'll take weeks!' complained Blanton.

The Supreme Intelligence turned on him fiercely.

'Well?' he demanded. He continued to stare for a moment, and Blanton wrinkled up in the baleful glow of his superior's scorn. 'And,' Detective Mallory added magnanimously, 'I will do the rest.'

Thus the campaign was planned against the Burglar and the Girl.

CHAPTER 4

Hutchinson Hatch was a newspaper reporter, a long, lean, hungry-looking young man with an insatiable appetite for facts. This last was, perhaps, an astonishing trait in a reporter; and Hatch was positively finicky on the point. That's why his City Editor believed in him. If Hatch had come in and told his City Editor that he had seen a blue elephant with pink side-whiskers his City Editor would have known that that elephant was blue – mentally, morally, physically, spiritually and everlastingly – not any washed-out green or purple, but blue.

Hatch was remarkable in other ways, too. For instance, he believed in the use of a little human intelligence in his profession. As a matter of fact, on several occasions he had demonstrated that it was really an excellent thing – human intelligence. His mind was well poised, his methods thorough, his style direct.

Along with dozens of others Hatch was at work on the Randolph robbery, and knew what the others knew – no more. He had studied the case so closely that he was beginning to believe, strangely enough, that perhaps the police were right in their theory as to the identity of the Burglar and the Girl – that is, that they were professional crooks. He could do a thing like that sometimes – bring his mind around to admit the possibility of somebody else being right.

It was on Saturday afternoon – two days after the Randolph affair – that Hatch was sitting in Detective Mallory's private office at Police Headquarters laboriously extracting from the Supreme Intelligence the precise things he had not found out about the robbery. The telephone-bell rang. Hatch got one end of the conversation – he couldn't help it. It was something like this: 'Hello!… Yes, Detective Mallory… Missing?… What's her name?… What?… Oh, Dorothy!… Yes?… Merritt?…Oh, Merryman!… Well, what the deuce is it then?… SPELL IT! … M-e-r-e-d-i-t-h. Why didn't you say that at first?… How long has she been gone? … Huh? … Thursday evening? … What does she look like? … Auburn hair. Red, you mean? … Oh, ruddy! I'd like to know what's the difference.'

The detective had drawn up a pad of paper and was jotting down what Hatch imagined to be the description of a missing girl. Then:

'Who is this talking?' asked the detective.

There was a little pause as he got the answer, and, having the answer, he whistled his astonishment, after which he glanced around quickly at the reporter, who was staring dreamily out a window.

'No,' said the Supreme Intelligence over the phone. 'It wouldn't be wise to make it public. It isn't necessary at all. I understand. I'll order a search immediately. No. The newspapers will get nothing of it. Goodbye.'

'A story?' inquired Hatch carelessly as the detective hung up the receiver.

'Doesn't amount to anything,' was the reply.

'Yes, that's obvious,' remarked the reporter drily.

'Well, whatever it is, it is not going to be made public,' retorted the Supreme Intelligence sharply. He never did like Hatch, anyway. 'It's one of those things that don't do any good in the newspapers, so I'll not let this one get there.'

Hatch yawned to show that he had no further interest in the matter, and went out. But there was the germ of an idea in his head which would have startled Detective Mallory, and he paced up and down outside to develop it. A girl missing!

A red-headed girl missing! A red-headed girl missing since Thursday! Thursday was the night of the Randolph masked ball. The missing Girl of the West was red-headed! Mallory had seemed astonished when he learned the name of the person who reported this last case! Therefore the person who reported it was high up – perhaps! Certainly high enough up to ask and receive the courtesy of police suppression – and the missing girl's name was Dorothy Meredith!

Hatch stood still for a long time on the curb and figured it out. Suddenly he rushed off to a telephone and called up Stuyvesant Randolph at Seven Oaks. He asked the first question with trepidation: 'Mr Randolph, can you give me the address of Miss Dorothy Meredith?'

'Miss Meredith?' came the answer. 'Let's see. I think she is stopping with the Morgan Greytons, at their suburban place.'

The reporter gulped down a shout. 'Worked, by thunder!' he exclaimed to himself. Then, in a deadly, forced calm: 'She attended the masked ball Thursday evening, didn't she?'

'Well, she was invited.'

'You didn't see her there?'

'No. Who is this?'

Then Hatch hung up the receiver. He was nearly choking with excitement, for, in addition to all those virtues which have been enumerated, he possessed, too, the quality of enthusiasm. It was no part of his purpose to tell anybody anything. Mallory didn't know, he was confident, anything of the girl having been a possible guest at the ball. And what Mallory didn't know now wouldn't be found out, all of which was a sad reflection upon the detective.

In this frame of mind Hatch started for the suburban place of the Greytons. He found the house without difficulty. Morgan Greyton – an aged gentleman of wealth and exclusive ideas – wasn't in. Hatch handed a card bearing only his name, to a maid, and after a few minutes Mrs Greyton appeared. She was a motherly, sweet-faced old lady of seventy, with that grave, exquisite courtesy which makes mere man feel ashamed of himself. Hatch had that feeling when he looked at her and thought of what he was going to ask.

'I came up direct from Police Headquarters,' he explained diplomatically, 'to learn any details you may be able to give us as to the disappearance of Miss Meredith.'

'Oh, yes,' replied Mrs Greyton. 'My husband said he was going to ask the police to look into the matter. It is most mysterious – most mysterious! We can't imagine where Dollie is, unless she has eloped. Do you know that idea keeps coming to me and won't go away?'

She spoke as if it were a naughty child.

'If you'll tell me something about Miss Meredith – who she is and all that?' Hatch suggested.

'Oh, yes, to be sure,' exclaimed Mrs. Greyton. 'Dollie is a distant cousin of my husband's sister's husband,' she explained precisely. 'She lives in Baltimore, but is visiting us. She has been here for several weeks. She's a dear, sweet girl, but I'm afraid – afraid she has eloped.'

The aged voice quivered a little, and Hatch was more ashamed of himself than ever.

'Some time ago she met a man named Herbert – Richard Herbert, I think, and –'

'Dick Herbert?' the reporter exclaimed suddenly.

'Do you know the young gentleman?' inquired the old lady eagerly.

'Yes, it just happens that we were classmates in Harvard,' said the reporter.

'And is he a nice young man?'

'A good, clean-cut, straightforward, decent man,' replied Hatch. He could speak with a certain enthusiasm about Dick Herbert. 'Go on, please,' he urged.

'Well, for some reason I don't know, Dollie's father objects to Mr Herbert's attentions to her – as a matter of fact, Mr Meredith has absolutely prohibited them – but she's a young, headstrong girl, and I fear that, although she had outwardly yielded to her father's wishes, she had clandestinely kept up a correspondence with Mr Herbert. Last Thursday evening she went out un-attended and since then we have not heard from her – not a word. We can only surmise – my husband and I – that they have eloped. I know her father and mother will be heartbroken, but I have always noticed that if a girl sets her heart on a man, she will get him. And perhaps it's just as well that she has eloped now since you assure me he is a nice young man.'

Hatch was choking back a question that rose in his throat. He hated to ask it, because he felt this dear, garrulous old woman would have hated him for it, if she could have known its purpose. But at last it came.

'Do you happen to know,' he asked, 'if Miss Meredith attended the Randolph ball at Seven Oaks on Thursday evening?'

'I dare say she received an invitation,' was the reply. 'She receives many invitations, but I don't think she went there. It was a costume affair, I suppose?'

The reporter nodded.

'Well, I hardly believe she went there then,' Mrs. Greyton replied. 'She has had no costume of any sort made. No, I am positive she has eloped with Mr Herbert, but I should like to hear from her to satisfy myself and explain to her parents. We did not permit Mr Herbert to come here, and it will be very hard to explain.'

Hatch heard the slight rustle of a skirt in the hall and glanced toward the door. No one appeared, and he turned back to Mrs Greyton.

'I don't suppose it possible that Miss Meredith has returned to Baltimore?' he asked.

'Oh, no!' was the positive reply. 'Her father there telegraphed to her today – I opened it – saying he would be here, probably tonight, and I – I haven't the heart to tell him the truth when he arrives. Somehow, I have been hoping that we would hear and – and –'

Then Hatch took his shame in his hand and excused himself. The maid attended him to the door.

'How much is it worth to you to know if Miss Meredith went to the masked ball?' asked the maid cautiously.

'Eavesdropping, eh?' asked Hatch in disgust.

The maid shrugged her shoulders.

'How much is it worth?' she repeated.

Hatch extended his hand. She took a ten-dollar bill which lay there and secreted it in some remote recess of her being.

'Miss Meredith did go to the ball,' she said. 'She went there to meet Mr Herbert. They had arranged to elope from there and she had made all her plans. I was in her confidence and assisted her.'

'What did she wear?' asked Hatch eagerly.

'Her costume was that of a Western Girl,' the maid responded. 'She wore a sombrero, and carried a Bowie knife and revolver.'

Hatch nearly swallowed his palate.

CHAPTER 5

Hatch started back to the city with his brain full of seven-column heads. He thoughtfully lighted a cigar just before he stepped on the car.

'No smoking,' said the conductor.

The reporter stared at him with dull eyes and then went in and sat down with the cigar in his mouth.

'No smoking, I told you,' bawled the conductor.

'Certainly not,' exclaimed Hatch indignantly. He turned and glared at the only other occupant of the car, a little girl. She wasn't smoking. Then he looked at the conductor and awoke suddenly.

'Miss Meredith is the girl,' Hatch was thinking. 'Mallory doesn't even dream it and never will. He won't send a man out there to do what I did. The Greytons are anxious to keep it quiet, and they won't say anything to anybody else until they know what really happened. I've got it bottled up, and don't know how to pull the cork. Now, the question is: What possible connection can there be between Dorothy Meredith and the Burglar? Was Dick Herbert the Burglar? Why, of course not! Then – what?'

Pondering all these things deeply, Hatch left the car and ran up to see Dick Herbert. He was too self-absorbed to notice that the blinds of the house were drawn. He rang, and after a long time a man-servant answered the bell.

'Mr Herbert here?' Hatch asked.

'Yes, sir, he's here,' replied the servant, 'but I don't know if he can see you. He is not very well, sir.'

'Not very well?' Hatch repeated.

'No, it's not that he's sick, sir. He was hurt and –'

'Who is it, Blair?' came Herbert's voice from the top of the

24

stair.

'Mr Hatch, sir.'

'Come up, Hatch!' Dick called cordially. 'Glad to see you. I'm so lonesome here I don't know what to do with myself.'

The reporter ran up the steps and into Dick's room.

'Not that one,' Dick smiled as Hatch reached for his right hand. 'It's out of business. Try this one –' And he offered his left.

'What's the matter?' Hatch inquired.

'Little hurt, that's all,' said Dick. 'Sit down. I got it knocked out the other night and I've been here in this big house alone with Blair ever since. The doctor told me not to venture out yet. It has been lonesome, too. All the folks are away, up in Nova Scotia, and took the other servants along. How are you, anyhow?'

Hatch sat down and stared at Dick thoughtfully. Herbert was a good-looking, forceful person of twenty-eight or thirty, and a corking right-guard. Now he seemed a little washed out, and there was a sort of pallor beneath the natural tan. He was a young man of family, unburdened by superlative wealth, but possessing in his own person the primary elements of success. He looked what Hatch had said of him: a 'good, clean-cut, straightforward, decent man'.

'I came up here to say something to you in my professional capacity,' the reporter began at last, 'and frankly, I don't know how to say it.'

Dick straightened up in his chair with a startled expression on his face. He didn't speak, but there was something in his eyes which interested Hatch immensely.

'Have you been reading the papers?' the reporter asked – 'that is, during the last couple of days?'

'Yes.'

'Of course, then, you've seen the stories about the Randolph robbery?'

Dick smiled a little.

'Yes,' he said. 'Clever, wasn't it?'

'It was,' Hatch responded enthusiastically. 'It was.' He was silent for a moment as he accepted and lighted a cigarette. 'It doesn't happen,' he went on, 'that, by any possible chance, you know anything about it, does it?'

'Not beyond what I saw in the papers. Why?'

'I'll be frank and ask you some questions, Dick,' Hatch resumed in a tone which betrayed his discomfort. 'Remember I am here in my official capacity – that is, not as a friend of yours, but as a reporter. You need not answer the questions if you don't want to.'

Dick arose with a little agitation in his manner and went over and stood beside the window.

'What is it all about?' he demanded. 'What are the questions?'

'Do you know where Miss Dorothy Meredith is?'

Dick turned suddenly and glared at him with a certain lowering of his eyebrows which Hatch knew from the football days.

'What about her?' he asked.

'Where is she?' Hatch insisted.

'At home, so far as I know. Why?'

'She is not there,' the reporter informed him, 'and the Greytons believe that you eloped with her.'

'Eloped with her?' Dick repeated. 'She is not at home?'

'No. She's been missing since Thursday evening – the evening of the Randolph affair. Mr Greyton has asked the police to look for her, and they are doing so now, but quietly. It is not known to the newspapers – that is, to other newspapers.

Your name has not been mentioned to the police. Now, isn't it a fact that you did intend to elope with her on Thursday evening?'

Dick strode feverishly across the room several times, then stopped in front of Hatch's chair.

'This isn't any silly joke?' he asked fiercely.

'Isn't it a fact that you did intend to elope with her on Thursday evening?' the reporter went on steadily.

'I won't answer that question.'

'Did you get an invitation to the Randolph ball?'

'Yes.'

'Did you go?'

Dick was staring straight down into his eyes.

'I won't answer that, either,' he said after a pause.

'Where were you on the evening of the masked ball?'

'Nor will I answer that.'

When the newspaper instinct is fully aroused a reporter has no friends. Hatch had forgotten that he ever knew Dick Herbert. To him the young man was now merely a thing from which he might wring certain information for the benefit of the palpitating public.

'Did the injury to your arm,' he went on after the approved manner of attorney for the prosecution, 'prevent you going to the ball?'

'I won't answer that.'

'What is the nature of the injury?'

'Now, see here, Hatch,' Dick burst out, and there was a dangerous undertone in his manner, 'I shall not answer any more questions – particularly that last one – unless I know what this is all about. Several things happened on the evening of the masked ball that I can't go over with you or anyone else, but as for me having any personal knowledge of events at the masked ball – well, you and I are not talking of the same thing at all.'

He paused, started to say something else, then changed his mind and was silent.

'Was it a pistol shot?' Hatch went on calmly.

Dick's lips were compressed to a thin line as he looked at the reporter, and he controlled himself only by an effort.

'Where did you get that idea?' he demanded.

Hatch would have hesitated a long time before he told him where he got that idea; but vaguely it had some connection with the fact that at least two shots were fired at the Burglar and the Girl when they raced away from Seven Oaks.

While the reporter was rummaging through his mind for an answer to the question there came a rap at the door and Blair appeared with a card. He handed it to Dick, who glanced at it, looked a little surprised, then nodded. Blair disappeared. After a moment there were footsteps on the stairs and Stuyvesant Randolph entered.

CHAPTER 6

Dick arose and offered his left hand to Mr Randolph, who calmly ignored it, turning his gaze instead upon the reporter.

'I had hoped to find you alone,' he said frostily.

Hatch made as if to rise.

'Sit still, Hatch,' Dick commanded. 'Mr Hatch is a friend of mine, Mr Randolph. I don't know what you want to say, but whatever it is, you may say it freely before him.'

Hatch knew that humour in Dick. It always preceded the psychological moment when he wanted to climb down someone's throat and open an umbrella. The tone was calm, the words clearly enunciated, and the face was white – whiter than it had been before.

'I shouldn't like to –' Mr Randolph began.

'You may say what you want to before Mr Hatch, or not at all, as you please,' Dick went on evenly.

Mr Randolph cleared his throat twice and waved his hands with an expression of resignation.

'Very well,' he replied. 'I have come to request the return of my gold plate.'

Hatch leaned forward in his chair, gripping its arms fiercely. This was a question bearing broadly on a subject that he wanted to mention, but he didn't know how. Mr Randolph apparently found it easy enough.

'What gold plate?' asked Dick steadily.

'The eleven pieces that you, in the garb of a Burglar, took from my house last Thursday evening,' said Mr Randolph. He was quite calm.

Dick took a sudden step forward, then straightened up with flushed face. His left hand closed with a snap and the nails bit into the flesh; the fingers of the helpless right hand worked nervously. In a minute now Hatch could see him climbing all over Mr Randolph.

But again Dick gained control of himself. It was a sort of recognition of the fact that Mr Randolph was fifty years old; Hatch knew it; Mr Randolph's knowledge on the subject didn't appear. Suddenly Dick laughed.

'Sit down, Mr Randolph, and tell me about it,' he suggested.

'It isn't necessary to go into details,' continued Mr Randolph, still standing. 'I had not wanted to go this far in the presence of a third person, but you forced me to do it. Now, will you or will you not return the plate?'

'Would you mind telling me just what makes you think I've got it?' Dick insisted.

'It is as simple as it is conclusive,' said Mr Randolph. 'You received an invitation to the masked ball. You went there in your Burglar garb and handed your invitation-card to my servant. He noticed you particularly and read your name on the card. He remembered that name perfectly. I was compelled to tell the story as I knew it to Detective Mallory. I did not mention your name; my servant remembered it, had given it to me in fact, but I forbade him to repeat it to the police. He told them something about having burned the invitation-cards.'

'Oh, wouldn't that please Mallory?' Hatch thought.

'I have not even intimated to the police that I have the least idea of your identity,' Mr Randolph went on, still standing. 'I had believed that it was some prank of yours and that the plate would be returned in due time. Certainly I could not account for you taking it in any other circumstances. My reticence, it is needless to say, was in consideration of your name and family. But now I want the plate. If it was a prank to carry out the *rôle* of the Burglar, it is time for it to end. If the fact that the matter is now in the hands of the police has frightened you into the seeming necessity of keeping the plate for the present to protect yourself, you may dismiss that. When the plate is returned to me I shall see that the police drop the matter.'

Dick had listened with absorbed interest. Hatch looked at him from time to time and saw only attention – not anger.

'And the Girl?' asked Dick at last. 'Does it happen that you have as cleverly traced her?'

'No,' Mr Randolph replied frankly. 'I haven't the faintest idea who she is. I suppose no one knows that but you. I have no interest further than to recover the plate. I may say that I called here yesterday, Friday, and asked to see you, but was informed that you had been hurt, so I went away to give you opportunity to recover somewhat.'

'Thanks,' said Dick drily. 'Awfully considerate.'

There was a long silence. Hatch was listening with all the multitudinous ears of a good reporter.

'Now the plate,' Mr Randolph suggested again impatiently. 'Do you deny that you got it?'

'I do,' replied Dick firmly.

'I was afraid you would, and, believe me, Mr Herbert, such a course is a mistaken one,' said Mr Randolph. 'I will give you twenty-four hours to change your mind. If, at the end of that time, you see fit to return the plate, I shall drop the matter and use my influence to have the police do so. If the plate is not returned I shall be compelled to turn over all the facts to the police with your name.'

'Is that all?' Dick demanded suddenly.

'Yes, I believe so.'

'Then get out of here before I –' Dick started forward, then dropped back into a chair.

Mr Randolph drew on his gloves and went out, closing the door behind him.

For a long time Dick sat there, seemingly oblivious of Hatch's presence, supporting his head with his left hand, while the right hung down loosely beside him. Hatch was inclined to be sympathetic, for, strange as it may seem, some reporters have even the human quality of sympathy – although there are persons who will not believe it.

'Is there anything I can do?' Hatch asked at last. 'Anything you want to say?'

'Nothing,' Dick responded wearily. 'Nothing. You may think what you like. There are, as I said, several things of which I cannot speak, even if it comes to a question – a question of having to face the charge of theft in open court. I simply can't say anything.'

'But – but –' stammered the reporter.

'Absolutely not another word,' said Dick firmly.

CHAPTER 7

Those satellites of the Supreme Police Intelligence of the Metropolitan District who had been taking the Randolph mystery to pieces to see what made it tick, lined up in front of Detective Mallory, in his private office, at police headquarters, early Saturday evening. They did not seem happy. The Supreme Intelligence placed his feet on the desk and glowered; that was a part of the job.

'Well, Downey?' he asked.

'I went out to Seven Oaks and got the automobile the Burglar left, as you instructed,' reported Downey. 'Then I started out to find its owner, or someone who knew it. It didn't have a number on it, so the job wasn't easy, but I found the owner all right, all right.'

Detective Mallory permitted himself to look interested.

'He lives at Merton, four miles from Seven Oaks,' Downey resumed. 'His name is Blake – William Blake. His auto was in the shed a hundred feet or so from his house on Thursday evening at nine o'clock. It wasn't there Friday morning.'

'Umph!' remarked Detective Mallory.

'There is no question but what Blake told me the truth,' Downey went on. 'To me it seems probable that the Burglar went out from the city to Merton by train, stole the auto and ran it on to Seven Oaks. That's all there seems to be to it. Blake proved ownership of the machine and I left it with him.'

The Supreme Intelligence chewed his cigar frantically.

'And the other machine?' he asked.

'I have here a bloodstained cushion, the back of a seat from the car in which the Burglar and the Girl escaped,' continued Downey in a walk-right-up-ladies-and-gentlemen sort of voice. 'I found the car late this afternoon at a garage in

Pleasantville. We knew, of course, that it belonged to Nelson Sharp, a guest at the masked ball. According to the manager of the garage the car was standing in front of his place this morning when he arrived to open up. The number had been removed.'

Detective Mallory examined the cushion which Downey handed to him. Several dark brown stains told the story – one of the occupants of the car had been wounded.

'Well, that's something,' commented the Supreme Intelligence. 'We know now that when Cunningham fired at least one of the persons in the car was hit, and we may make our search accordingly. The Burglar and the Girl probably left the car where it was found during the preceding night.'

'It seems so,' said Downey. 'I shouldn't think they would have dared to keep it long. Autos of that size and power are too easily traced. I asked Mr Sharp to run down and identify the car and he did so. The stains were new.'

The Supreme Intelligence digested that in silence while his satellites studied his face, seeking some inkling of the convolutions of that marvellous mind.

'Very good, Downey,' said Detective Mallory at last. 'Now Cunningham?'

'Nothing,' said Cunningham in shame and sorrow. 'Nothing.'

'Didn't you find anything at all about the premises?'

'Nothing,' repeated Cunningham. 'The Girl left no wrap at Seven Oaks. None of the servants remembers having seen her in the room where the wraps were checked. I searched all around the place and found a dent in the ground under the smoking room window, where the gold plate had been thrown, and there were what seemed to be footprints in the grass, but it was all nothing.'

'We can't arrest a dent and footprints,' said the Supreme Intelligence cuttingly.

The satellites laughed sadly. It was part of the deference they owed to the Supreme Intelligence.

'And you, Blanton?' asked Mr Mallory. 'What did you do with the list of guests?'

'I haven't got a good start yet,' responded Blanton hopelessly. 'There are 360 names on the list. I have been able to see possibly thirty. It's worse than making a city directory. I won't be through for a month. Randolph and his wife checked off a large number of these whom they knew were there. The others I am looking up as rapidly as I can.'

The detectives sat moodily thoughtful for uncounted minutes. Finally Detective Mallory broke the silence: 'There seems to be no question but that any clue that might have come from either of the automobiles is disposed of unless it is the fact that we now know one of the thieves was wounded. I readily see how the theft could have been committed by a man as bold as this fellow. Now we must concentrate all our efforts to running down the invited guests and learning just where they were that evening. All of you will have to get on this job and hustle it. We know that the Burglar did present an invitation-card with a name on it.'

The detectives went their respective ways and then Detective Mallory deigned to receive representatives of the press, among them Hutchinson Hatch. Hatch was worried. He knew a whole lot of things, but they didn't do him any good. He felt that he could print nothing as it stood, yet he would not tell the police, because that would give it to everyone else, and he had a picture of how the Supreme Intelligence would tangle it if he got hold of it.

'Well, boys,' said Detective Mallory smilingly, when the press filed in, 'there's nothing to say. Frankly, I will tell you that we have not been able to learn anything – at least anything that can be given out. You know, of course, about the finding of the two automobiles that figured in the case, and the bloodstained cushion?'

The press nodded collectively.

'Well, that's all there is yet. My men are still at work, but I'm a little afraid the gold plate will never be found. It has probably been melted up. The cleverness of the thieves you can judge for yourself by the manner in which they handled the automobiles.'

And yet Hatch was not surprised when, late that night, Police Headquarters made known the latest sensation. This was a bulletin, based on a telephone message from Stuyvesant Randolph to the effect that the gold plate had been returned by express to Seven Oaks. This mystified the police beyond description; but official mystification was as nothing to Hatch's state of mind. He knew of the scene in Dick Herbert's room and remembered Mr Randolph's threat.

'Then Dick did have the plate,' he told himself.

Whole flocks of detectives, reporters, and newspaper artists appeared at Seven Oaks early next morning. It had been too late to press an investigation the night before. The newspapers had only time telephonically to confirm the return of the plate. Now the investigators unanimously voiced one sentiment: 'Show us!'

Hatch arrived in the party headed by Detective Mallory, with Downey and Cunningham trailing. Blanton was off somewhere with his little list, presumably still at it. Mr Randolph had not come down to breakfast when the investigators arrived, but had given his servant permission to exhibit the plate, the wrappings in which it had come, and the string wherewith it had been tied.

The plate arrived in a heavy cardboard box, covered twice over with a plain piece of stiff brown paper, which had no markings save the address and the 'paid' stamp of the express company. Detective Mallory devoted himself first to the address. It was:

Mr Stuyvesant Randolph,
'Seven Oaks',
via Merton.

In the upper left-hand corner were scribbled the words:

From John Smith,
State Street,
Watertown.

Detectives Mallory, Downey, and Cunningham studied the handwriting on the paper minutely.

'It's a man's,' said Detective Downey.

'It's a woman's,' said Detective Cunningham.

'It's a child's,' said Detective Mallory.

'Whatever it is, it is disguised,' said Hatch.

He was inclined to agree with Detective Cunningham that it was a woman's purposely altered, and in that event – Great Caesar! There came that flock of seven-column heads again! And he couldn't open the bottle!

The simple story of the arrival of the gold plate at Seven Oaks was told thrillingly by the servant.

'It was eight o'clock last night,' he said. 'I was standing in the hall here. Mr and Mrs Randolph were still at the dinner table. They dined alone. Suddenly I heard the sound of wagon-wheels on the granolithic road in front of the house. I listened intently. Yes, it was wagon-wheels.'

The detectives exchanged significant glances.

'I heard the wagon stop,' the servant went on in an awed tone. 'Still I listened. Then came the sound of footsteps on the walk and then on the steps. I walked slowly along the hall toward the front door. As I did so the bell rang.'

'Yes, ting-a-ling-a-ling, we know. Go on,' Hatch interrupted impatiently.

'I opened the door,' the servant continued. 'A man stood there with a package. He was a burly fellow. 'Mr Randolph live here?' he asked gruffly. 'Yes,' I said. 'Here's a package for him,' said the man. 'Sign here.' I took the package and signed a book he gave me, and – and –'

'In other words,' Hatch interrupted again, 'an expressman brought the package here, you signed for it, and he went away?'

The servant stared at him haughtily.

'Yes, that's it,' he said coldly.

A few minutes later Mr Randolph in person appeared. He glanced at Hatch with a little surprise in his manner, nodded curtly, then turned to the detectives.

He could not add to the information the servant had given. His plate had been returned, prepaid. The matter was at an end so far as he was concerned. There seemed to be no need of further investigation.

'How about the jewelry that was stolen from your other guests?' demanded Detective Mallory.

'Of course, there's that,' said Mr Randolph. 'It had passed out of my mind.'

'Instead of being at an end this case has just begun,' the detective declared emphatically.

Mr Randolph seemed to have no further interest in the matter. He started out, then turned back at the door, and made a slight motion to Hatch which the reporter readily understood. As a result Hatch and Mr Randolph were closeted together in a small room across the hall a few minutes later.

'May I ask your occupation, Mr Hatch?' inquired Mr Randolph.

'I'm a reporter,' was the reply.

'A reporter?' Mr Randolph seemed surprised. 'Of course, when I saw you in Mr Herbert's rooms,' he went on after a little pause, 'I met you only as his friend. You saw what happened there. Now, may I ask you what you intend to publish about this affair?'

Hatch considered the question a moment. There seemed to be no objection to telling.

'I can't publish anything until I know everything, or until the police act,' he confessed frankly. 'I had been talking to Dick Herbert in a general way about this case when you arrived yesterday. I knew several things, or thought I did, that the police do not even suspect. But, of course, I can print only just what the police know and say.'

'I'm glad of that – very glad of it,' said Mr Randolph. 'It seems to have been a freak of some sort on Mr Herbert's part, and, candidly, I can't understand it. Of course he returned the plate, as I knew he would.'

'Do you really believe he is the man who came here as the Burglar?' asked Hatch curiously.

'I should not have done what you saw me do if I had not been absolutely certain,' Mr Randolph explained. 'One of the things, particularly, that was called to my attention – I don't know that you know of it – is the fact that the Burglar had a cleft in his chin. You know, of course, that Mr Herbert has such a cleft. Then there is the invitation-card with his name. Everything together makes it conclusive.'

Mr Randolph and the reporter shook hands. Three hours later the press and police had uncovered the Watertown end of the mystery as to how the express package had been sent. It was explained by the driver of an express wagon there and absorbed by greedily listening ears.

'The boss told me to call at No. 410 State Street and get a bundle,' the driver explained. 'I think somebody telephoned to him to send the wagon. I went up there yesterday morning. It's a small house, back a couple of hundred feet from the street, and has a stone fence around it. I opened the gate, went in, and rang the bell.

'No one answered the first ring, and I rang again. Still nobody answered and I tried the door. It was locked. I walked around the house, thinking there might be somebody in the back, but it was all locked up. I figured as how the folks that had telephoned for me wasn't in, and started out to my wagon, intending to stop by later.

'Just as I got to the gate, going out, I saw a package set down inside, hidden from the street behind the stone fence, with a dollar bill on it. I just naturally looked at it. It was the package directed to Mr Randolph. I reasoned as how the folks who phoned had to go out and left the package, so I took it along. I made out a receipt to John Smith, the name that was in the corner, and pinned it to a post, took the package and the money and went along. That's all.'

'You don't know if the package was there when you went in?' he was asked.

'I dunno. I didn't look. I couldn't help but see it when I came out, so I took it.'

Then the investigators sought out 'the boss'.

'Did the person who phoned give you a name?' inquired Detective Mallory.

'No, I didn't ask for one.'

'Was it a man or a woman talking?'

'A man,' was the unhesitating reply. 'He had a deep, heavy voice.'

The investigators trailed away, dismally despondent, toward No. 410 State Street. It was unoccupied; inquiry showed that it had been unoccupied for months. The Supreme Intelligence picked the lock and the investigators walked in, craning their necks. They expected, at the least, to find a thieves' rendezvous. There was nothing but dirt, and dust, and grime. Then the investigators returned to the city. They had found only that the gold plate had been returned, and they knew that when they started.

Hatch went home and sat down with his head in his hands to add up all he didn't know about the affair. It was surprising how much there was of it.

'Dick Herbert either did or didn't go to the ball,' he

soliloquised. 'Something happened to him that evening. He either did or didn't steal the gold plate, and every circumstance indicates that he did – which, of course, he didn't. Dorothy Meredith either was or was not at the ball. The maid's statement shows that she was, yet no one there recognised her – which indicates that she wasn't. She either did or didn't run away with somebody in an automobile. Anyhow, something happened to her, because she's missing. The gold plate is stolen, and the gold plate is back. I know that, thank Heaven! And now, knowing more about this affair than any other single individual, I don't know anything.'

Part 2:
The Girl and the Plate

CHAPTER 1

Low-bent over the steering-wheel, the Burglar sent the auto-mobile scuttling breathlessly along the flat road away from Seven Oaks. At the first shot he crouched down in the seat, dragging the Girl with him; at the second, he winced a little and clenched his teeth tightly. The car's headlights cut a dazzling pathway through the shadows, and trees flitted by as a solid wall. The shouts of pursuers were left behind, and still the Girl clung to his arm.

'Don't do that,' he commanded abruptly. 'You'll make me smash into something.'

'Why, Dick, they shot at us!' she protested indignantly.

The Burglar glanced at her, and, when he turned his eyes to the smooth road again, there was a flicker of a smile about the set lips.

'Yes, I had some such impression myself,' he acquiesced grimly.

'Why, they might have killed us!' the Girl went on.

'It is just barely possible that they had some such absurd idea when they shot,' replied the Burglar. 'Guess you never got caught in a pickle like this before?'

'I certainly never did!' replied the Girl emphatically.

The whir and grind of their car drowned other sounds – sounds from behind – but from time to time the Burglar looked back, and from time to time he let out a new notch in the speed-regulator. Already the pace was terrific, and the Girl bounced up and down beside him at each trivial irregularity in the road, while she clung frantically to the seat.

'Is it necessary to go so awfully fast?' she gasped at last.

The wind was beating on her face, her mask blew this way and that; the beribboned sombrero clung frantically to a fast-failing strand of ruddy hair. She clutched at the hat and saved it, but her hair tumbled down about her shoulders, a mass of gold, and floated out behind.

'Oh,' she chattered, 'I can't keep my hat on!'

The Burglar took another quick look behind, then his foot went out against the speed-regulator and the car fairly leaped with suddenly increased impetus. The regulator was in the last notch now, and the car was one that had raced at Ormond Beach.

'Oh, dear!' exclaimed the Girl again. 'Can't you go a little slower?'

'Look behind,' directed the Burglar tersely.

She glanced back and gave a little cry. Two giant eyes stared at her from a few hundred yards away as another car swooped along in pursuit, and behind this ominously glittering pair was still another.

'They're chasing us, aren't they?'

'They are,' replied the Burglar grimly, 'but if these tires hold, they haven't got a chance. A breakdown would –' He didn't finish the sentence. There was a sinister note in his voice, but the Girl was still looking back and did not heed it. To her excited imagination it seemed that the giant eyes behind were creeping up, and again she clutched the Burglar's arm.

'Don't do that, I say,' he commanded again.

'But, Dick, they mustn't catch us – they mustn't!'

'They won't.'

'But if they should –'

'They won't,' he repeated.

'It would be perfectly awful!'

'Worse than that.'

For a time the Girl silently watched him bending over the wheel, and a singular feeling of security came to her. Then the

46

car swept around a bend in the road, careening perilously, and the glaring eyes were lost. She breathed more freely.

'I never knew you handled an auto so well,' she said admiringly.

'I do lots of things people don't know I do,' he replied. 'Are those lights still there?'

'No, thank goodness!'

The Burglar touched a lever with his left hand and the whir of the machine became less pronounced. After a moment it began to slow down. The Girl noticed it and looked at him with new apprehension.

'Oh, we're stopping!' she exclaimed.

'I know it.'

They ran on for a few hundred feet; then the Burglar set the brake and, after a deal of jolting, the car stopped. He leaped out and ran around behind. As the Girl watched him uneasily there came a sudden crash and the auto trembled a little.

'What is it?' she asked quickly.

'I smashed that tail lamp,' he answered. 'They can see it, and it's too easy for them to follow.'

He stamped on the shattered fragments in the road, then came around to the side to climb in again, extending his left hand to the Girl.

'Quick, give me your hand,' he requested.

She did so wonderingly and he pulled himself into the seat beside her with a perceptible effort. The car shivered, then started on again, slowly at first, but gathering speed each moment. The Girl was staring at her companion curiously, anxiously.

'Are you hurt?' she asked at last.

He did not answer at the moment, not until the car had regained its former speed and was hurtling headlong through the night.

'My right arm's out of business,' he explained briefly, then: 'I got that second bullet in the shoulder.'

'Oh, Dick, Dick,' she exclaimed, 'and you hadn't said anything about it! You need assistance!'

A sudden rush of sympathy caused her to lay her hands again on his left arm. He shook them off roughly with something like anger in his manner.

'Don't do that!' he commanded for the third time. 'You'll make me smash hell out of this car.'

Startled by the violence of his tone, she recoiled dumbly, and the car swept on. As before, the Burglar looked back from time to time, but the lights did not reappear. For a long time the Girl was silent and finally he glanced at her.

'I beg your pardon,' he said humbly. 'I didn't mean to speak so sharply, but – but it's true.'

'It's really of no consequence,' she replied coldly. 'I am sorry – very sorry.'

'Thank you,' he replied.

'Perhaps it might be as well for you to stop the car and let me out,' she went on after a moment.

The Burglar either didn't hear or wouldn't heed. The dim lights of a small village rose up before them, then faded away again; a dog barked lonesomely beside the road. The streaming lights of their car revealed a tangle of crossroads just ahead, offering a definite method of shaking off pursuit. Their car swerved widely, and the Burglar's attention was centred on the road ahead.

'Does your arm pain you?' asked the Girl at last timidly.

'No,' he replied shortly. 'It's a sort of numbness. I'm afraid I'm losing blood, though.'

'Hadn't we better go back to the village and see a doctor?'

'Not this evening,' he responded promptly in a tone which she did not understand. 'I'll stop somewhere soon and bind it up.'

At last, when the village was well behind, the car came to a dark little road which wandered off aimlessly through a wood, and the Burglar slowed down to turn into it. Once in the shelter of the overhanging branches they proceeded slowly for a hundred yards or more, finally coming to a standstill.

'We must do it here,' he declared.

He leaped from the car, stumbled and fell. In an instant the Girl was beside him. The reflected light from the auto showed her dimly that he was trying to rise, showed her the pallor of his face where the chin below the mask was visible.

'I'm afraid it's pretty bad,' he said weakly. Then he fainted.

The Girl, stooping, raised his head to her lap and pressed her lips to his feverishly, time after time.

'Dick, Dick!' she sobbed, and tears fell upon the Burglar's sinister mask.

When the Burglar awoke to consciousness he was as near heaven as any mere man ever dares expect to be. He was comfortable – quite comfortable – wrapped in a delicious, languorous lassitude which forbade him opening his eyes to realisation. A woman's hand lay on his forehead, caressingly, and dimly he knew that another hand cuddled cosily in one of his own. He lay still, trying to remember, before he opened his eyes. Someone beside him breathed softly, and he listened, as if to music.

Gradually the need of action – just what action and to what purpose did not occur to him – impressed itself on his mind. He raised the disengaged hand to his face and touched the mask, which had been pushed back on his forehead. Then he recalled the ball, the shot, the chase, the hiding in the woods. He opened his eyes with a start. Utter darkness lay about him – for a moment he was not certain whether it was the darkness of blindness or of night.

'Dick, are you awake?' asked the Girl softly. He knew the voice and was content.

'Yes,' he answered languidly.

He closed his eyes again and some strange, subtle perfume seemed to envelop him. He waited. Warm lips were pressed to his own, thrilling him strangely, and the Girl rested a soft cheek against his.

'We have been very foolish, Dick,' she said, sweetly chiding, after a moment. 'It was all my fault for letting you expose yourself to danger, but I didn't dream of such a thing as this happening. I shall never forgive myself, because –'

'But –' he began protestingly.

'Not another word about it now,' she hurried on. 'We must go very soon. How do you feel?'

50

'I'm all right, or will be in a minute,' he responded, and he made as if to rise. 'Where is the car?'

'Right here. I extinguished the lights and managed to stop the engine for fear those horrid people who were after us might notice.'

'Good girl!'

'When you jumped out and fainted I jumped out, too. I'm afraid I was not very clever, but I managed to bind your arm. I took my handkerchief and pressed it against the wound after ripping your coat, then I bound it there. It stopped the flow of blood, but, Dick, dear, you must have medical attention just as soon as possible.'

The Burglar moved his shoulder a little and winced.

'Just as soon as I did that,' the Girl went on, 'I made you comfortable here on a cushion from the car.'

'Good girl!' he said again.

'Then I sat down to wait until you got better. I had no stimulant or anything, and I didn't dare to leave you, so – so I just waited,' she ended with a weary little sigh.

'How long was I knocked out?' he queried.

'I don't know; half an hour, perhaps.'

'The bag is all right, I suppose?'

'The bag?'

'The bag with the stuff – the one I threw in the car when we started?'

'Oh, yes, I suppose so! Really, I hadn't thought of it.'

'Hadn't thought of it?' repeated the Burglar, and there was a trace of astonishment in his voice. 'By George, you're a wonder!' he added.

He started to get on his feet, then dropped back weakly.

'Say, girlie,' he requested, 'see if you can find the bag in the car there and hand it out. Let's take a look.'

'Where is it?'

'Somewhere in front. I felt it at my feet when I jumped out.'

There was a rustle of skirts in the darkness, and after a moment a faint muffled clank as of one heavy metal striking dully against another.

'Goodness!' exclaimed the Girl. 'It's heavy enough. What's in it?'

'What's in it?' repeated the Burglar, and he chuckled. 'A fortune, nearly. It's worth being punctured for. Let me see.'

In the darkness he took the bag from her hands and fumbled with it a moment. She heard the metallic sound again and then several heavy objects were poured out on the ground.

'A good fourteen pounds of pure gold,' commented the Burglar. 'By George, I haven't but one match, but we'll see what it's like.'

The match was struck, sputtered for a moment, then flamed up, and the Girl, standing, looked down upon the Burglar on his knees beside a heap of gold plate. She stared at the glittering mass as if fascinated, and her eyes opened wide.

'Why, Dick, what is that?' she asked.

'It's Randolph's plate,' responded the Burglar complacently. 'I don't know how much it's worth, but it must be several thousands, on dead weight.'

'What are you doing with it?'

'What am I doing with it?' repeated the Burglar. He was about to look up when the match burned his finger and he dropped it. 'That's a silly question.'

'But how came it in your possession?' the Girl insisted.

'I acquired it by the simple act of – of dropping it into a bag and bringing it along. That and you in the same evening –' He stretched out a hand toward her, but she was not there.

He chuckled a little as he turned and picked up eleven plates, one by one, and replaced them in the bag.

'Nine – ten – eleven,' he counted. 'What luck did you have?'

'Dick Herbert, explain to me, please, what you are doing with that gold plate?' There was an imperative command in the voice.

The Burglar paused and rubbed his chin thoughtfully.

'Oh, I'm taking it to have it fixed!' he responded lightly.

'Fixed? Taking it this way at this time of the night?'

'Sure,' and he laughed pleasantly.

'You mean you – you – you stole it?' The words came with an effort.

'Well, I'd hardly call it that,' remarked the Burglar. 'That's a harsh word. Still, it's in my possession; it wasn't given to me, and I didn't buy it. You may draw your own conclusions.'

The bag lay beside him and his left hand caressed it idly, lovingly. For a long time there was silence.

'What luck did you have?' he asked again.

There was a startled gasp, a gurgle and accusing indignation in the Girl's low, tense voice.

'You – you stole it!'

'Well, if you prefer it that way – yes.'

The Burglar was staring steadily into the darkness toward that point whence came the voice, but the night was so dense that not a trace of the Girl was visible. He laughed again.

'It seems to me it was lucky I decided to take it at just this time and in these circumstances,' he went on tauntingly – 'lucky for you, I mean. If I hadn't been there you would have been caught.'

Again came the startled gasp.

'What's the matter?' demanded the Burglar sharply, after another silence. 'Why don't you say something?'

He was still peering unseeingly into the darkness. The bag of gold plate moved slightly under his hand. He opened his fingers to close them more tightly. It was a mistake. The bag was drawn away; his hand grasped – air.

'Stop that game now!' he commanded angrily. 'Where are you?'

He struggled to his feet. His answer was the crackling of a twig to his right. He started in that direction and brought up with a bump against the automobile. He turned, still groping blindly, and embraced a tree with undignified fervour. To his left he heard another slight noise and ran that way. Again he struck an obstacle. Then he began to say things, expressive things, burning things from the depths of an impassioned soul. The treasure had gone – disappeared into the shadows. The Girl was gone. He called, there was no answer. He drew his revolver fiercely, as if to fire it; then reconsidered and flung it down angrily.

'And I thought I had nerve!' he declared. It was a compliment.

CHAPTER 3

Extravagantly brilliant the sun popped up out of the east – not an unusual occurrence – and stared unblinkingly down upon a country road. There were the usual twittering birds and dew-spangled trees and nodding wild-flowers; also a dust that was shoe-top deep. The dawny air stirred lazily and rustling leaves sent long, sinuous shadows scampering back and forth.

Looking upon it all without enthusiasm or poetic exaltation was a Girl – a pretty Girl – a very pretty Girl. She sat on a stone beside the yellow roadway, a picture of weariness. A rough burlap sack, laden heavily, yet economically as to space, wallowed in the dust beside her. Her hair was tawny gold, and rebellious strands drooped listlessly about her face. A beribboned sombrero lay in her lap, supplementing a certain air of dilapidated bravado, due in part to a short skirt, heavy gloves and boots, a belt with a knife and revolver.

A robin, perched impertinently on a stump across the road, examined her at his leisure. She stared back at Signor Redbreast, and for this recognition he warbled a little song.

'I've a good mind to cry!' exclaimed the Girl suddenly.

Shamed and startled, the robin flew away. A mistiness came into the Girl's blue eyes and lingered there a moment, then her white teeth closed tightly and the glimmer of outraged emotion passed.

'Oh,' she sighed again, 'I'm so tired and hungry and I just know I'll never get anywhere at all!'

But despite the expressed conviction she arose and straightened up as if to resume her journey, turning to stare down at the bag. It was an unsightly symbol of blasted hopes, man's perfidy, crushed aspirations and – Heaven only knows what besides.

'I've a good mind to leave you right there,' she remarked to the bag spitefully. 'Perhaps I might hide it.' She considered the question. 'No, that wouldn't do. I must take it with me – and – and – Oh, Dick! Dick! What in the world was the matter with you, anyway?'

Then she sat down again and wept. The robin crept back to look and modestly hid behind a leaf. From this coign of vantage he watched her as she again arose and plodded off through the dust with the bag swinging over one shoulder. At last – there is an at last to everything – a small house appeared from behind a clump of trees. The Girl looked with incredulous eyes. It was really a house. Really! A tiny curl of smoke hovered over the chimney.

'Well, thank goodness, I'm somewhere, anyhow,' she declared with her first show of enthusiasm. 'I can get a cup of coffee or something.'

She covered the next fifty yards with a new spring in her leaden heels and with a new and firmer grip on the precious bag. Then – she stopped.

'Gracious!' and perplexed lines suddenly wrinkled her brow. 'If I should go in there with a pistol and a knife they'll think I was a brigand – or – or a thief, and I suppose I am,' she added as she stopped and rested the bag on the ground. 'At least I have stolen goods in my possession. Now, what shall I say if they ask questions? What am I? They wouldn't believe me if I told them really. Short skirt, boots and gloves: I know! I'm a bicyclist. My wheel broke down, and –'

Whereupon she gingerly removed the revolver from her belt and flung it into the underbrush – not at all in the direction she had intended – and the knife followed to keep it company. Having relieved herself of these sinister things, she straightened her hat, pushed back the rebellious hair, yanked at her skirt, and walked bravely up to the little house.

An Angel lived there – an Angel in a dizzily beflowered wrapper and a crabbed exterior. She listened to a rapidly constructed and wholly inconsistent story of a bicycle accident, which ended with a plea for a cup of coffee. Silently she proceeded to prepare it. After the pot was bubbling cheerfully and eggs had been put on and biscuits thrust into a stove to be warmed over, the Angel sat down at the table opposite the Girl.

'Book agent?' she asked.

'Oh, no!' replied the Girl.

'Sewing-machines?'

'No.'

There was a pause as the Angel settled and poured a cup of coffee.

'Make to order, I s'pose?'

'No,' the Girl replied uncertainly.

'What do you sell?'

'Nothing, I – I –' She stopped.

'What you got in the bag?' the Angel persisted.

'Some – some – just some – stuff,' stammered the Girl, and her face suddenly flushed crimson.

'What kind of stuff?'

The Girl looked into the frankly inquisitive eyes and was overwhelmed by a sense of her own helplessness. Tears started, and one pearly drop ran down her perfect nose and splashed in the coffee. That was the last straw. She leaned forward suddenly with her head on her arms and wept.

'Please, please don't ask questions!' she pleaded. 'I'm a poor, foolish, helpless, misguided, disillusioned woman!'

'Yes'm,' said the Angel. She took up the eggs, then came over and put a kindly arm about the Girl's shoulders. 'There, there!'

she said soothingly. 'Don't take on like that! Drink some coffee, and eat a bite, and you'll feel better!'

'I have had no sleep at all and no food since yesterday, and I've walked miles and miles and miles,' the Girl rushed on feverishly. 'It's all because – because –' She stopped suddenly.

'Eat something,' commanded the Angel.

The Girl obeyed. The coffee was weak and muddy and delightful; the biscuits were yellow and lumpy and delicious; the eggs were eggs. The Angel sat opposite and watched the Girl as she ate.

'Husband beat you?' she demanded suddenly.

The Girl blushed and nearly choked on a biscuit.

'No,' she hastened to say. 'I have no husband.'

'Well, there ain't no serious trouble in this world till you marry a man that beats you,' said the Angel judicially. It was the final word.

The Girl didn't answer, and, in view of the fact that she had sufficient data at hand to argue the point, this repression required heroism. Perhaps she will never get credit for it. She finished the breakfast in silence and leaned back with some measure of returning content in her soul.

'In a hurry?' asked the Angel.

'No. I have no place to go. What is the nearest village or town?'

'Watertown, but you'd better stay and rest a while. You look all tuckered out.'

'Oh, thank you so much,' said the Girl gratefully. 'But it would be so much trouble for –'

The Angel picked up the burlap bag, shook it inquiringly, then started toward the short stairs leading up.

'Please, please!' exclaimed the Girl suddenly. 'I – I – let me have that, please!'

The Angel relinquished the bag without a word. The Girl took it, tremblingly, then, suddenly dropping it, clasped the Angel in her arms and placed upon her unresponsive lips a kiss for which a mere man would have endangered his immortal soul. The Angel wiped her mouth with the back of her hand and went on up the stairs with the Girl following.

For a time the Girl lay, with wet eyes, on a clean little bed, thinking. Humiliation, exhaustion, man's perfidy, disillusionment, and the kindness of an utter stranger all occupied her until she fell asleep. Then she was chased by a policeman with automobile lights for eyes, and there was a parade of hard-boiled eggs and yellow, lumpy biscuits.

When she awoke the room was quite dark. She sat up a little bewildered at first; then she remembered. After a moment she heard the voice of the Angel, below. It rippled on querulously; then she heard the gruff voice of a man.

'Diamond rings?'

The Girl sat up in bed and listened intently. Involuntarily her hands were clasped together. Her rings were still safe. The Angel's voice went on for a moment again.

'Something in a bag?' inquired the man.

Again the Angel spoke.

Terror seized upon the Girl; imagination ran riot, and she rose from the bed, trembling. She groped about the dark room noiselessly. Every shadow lent her new fears. Then from below came the sound of heavy footsteps. She listened fearfully. They came on toward the stairs, then paused. A match was struck and the step sounded on the stairs.

After a moment there was a knock at the door, a pause, then another knock. Finally the door was pushed open and a huge figure – the figure of a man – appeared, sheltering a candle with one hand. He peered about the room as if perplexed.

'Ain't nobody up here,' he called gruffly down the stairs.

There was a sound of hurrying feet and the Angel entered, her face distorted by the flickering candlelight.

'For the land's sakes!' she exclaimed.

'Went away without even saying thank you,' grumbled the man. He crossed the room and closed a window. 'You ain't got no better sense than a chicken,' he told the Angel. 'Take in anybody that comes.'

CHAPTER 4

If Willie's little brother hadn't had a pain in his tummy this story might have gone by other and devious ways to a different conclusion. But fortunately he did have, so it happened that at precisely 8.47 o'clock of a warm evening Willie was racing madly along a side street of Watertown, drugstore-bound, when he came face to face with a Girl – a pretty Girl – a very pretty Girl. She was carrying a bag that clanked a little at each step.

'Oh, little boy!' she called.

'Hunh?' and Willie stopped so suddenly that he endangered his equilibrium, although that isn't how he would have said it.

'Nice little boy,' said the Girl soothingly, and she patted his tousled head while he gnawed a thumb in pained embarrassment. 'I'm very tired. I have been walking a great distance. Could you tell me, please, where a lady, unattended, might get a night's lodging somewhere near here?'

'Hunh?' gurgled Willie through the thumb.

Wearily the Girl repeated it all and at its end Willie giggled. It was the most exasperating incident of a long series of exasperating incidents, and the Girl's grip on the bag tightened a little. Willie never knew how nearly he came to being hammered to death with fourteen pounds of solid gold.

'Well?' inquired the Girl at last.

'Dunno,' said Willie. 'Jimmy's got the stomach-ache,' he added irrelevantly.

'Can't you think of a hotel or boarding house nearby?' the Girl insisted.

'Dunno,' replied Willie. 'I'm going to the drugstore for a pair o' gorrick.'

The Girl bit her lip, and that act probably saved Willie from the dire consequences of his unconscious levity, for after a moment the Girl laughed aloud.

'Where is the drugstore?' she asked.

'Round the corner. I'm going.'

'I'll go along, too, if you don't mind,' the Girl said, and she turned and walked beside him. Perhaps the drug clerk would be able to illuminate the situation.

'I swallyed a penny oncst,' Willie confided suddenly.

'Too bad!' commented the Girl.

'Unh unnh,' Willie denied emphatically. ''Cause when I cried, Paw gimme a quarter.' He was silent a moment, then: 'If I'd 'a' swallyed that, I reckin he'd a gimme a dollar. Gee!'

This is the optimism that makes the world go round. The philosophy took possession of the Girl and cheered her. When she entered the drugstore she walked with a lighter step and there was a trace of a smile about her pretty mouth. A clerk, the only attendant, came forward.

'I want a pair o' gorrick,' Willie announced.

The Girl smiled, and the clerk, paying no attention to the boy, went toward her.

'Better attend to him first,' she suggested. 'It seems urgent.'

The clerk turned to Willie.

'Paregoric?' he inquired. 'How much?'

'About a quart, I reckin,' replied the boy. 'Is that enough?'

'Quite enough,' commented the clerk. He disappeared behind the prescription screen and returned after a moment with a small phial. The boy took it, handed over a coin, and went out, whistling. The Girl looked after him with a little longing in her eyes.

'Now, madam?' inquired the clerk suavely.

'I only want some information,' she replied. 'I was out on my bicycle' – she gulped a little – 'when it broke down, and I'll have to remain here in town overnight, I'm afraid. Can you direct me to a quiet hotel or boarding house where I might stay?'

'Certainly,' replied the clerk briskly. 'The Stratford, just a block up this street. Explain the circumstances, and it will be all right, I'm sure.'

The Girl smiled at him again and cheerfully went her way. That small boy had been a leaven to her drooping spirits. She found the Stratford without difficulty and told the usual bicycle lie, with a natural growth of detail and a burning sense of shame. She registered as Elizabeth Carlton and was shown to a modest little room.

Her first act was to hide the gold plate in the closet; her second was to take it out and hide it under the bed. Then she sat down on a couch to think. For an hour or more she considered the situation in all its hideous details, planning her desolate future – women like to plan desolate futures – then her eye chanced to fall upon an afternoon paper, which, with glaring headlines, announced the theft of the Randolph gold plate. She read it. It told, with startling detail, things that had and had not happened in connection therewith.

This comprehended in all its horror, she promptly arose and hid the bag between the mattress and the springs. Soon after she extinguished the light and retired with little shivers running up and down all over her. She snuggled her head down under the cover. She didn't sleep much – she was still thinking – but when she arose next morning her mind was made up.

First she placed the eleven gold plates in a heavy cardboard box, then she bound it securely with brown paper and twine and addressed it: 'Stuyvesant Randolph, Seven Oaks, via Merton'. She had sent express packages before and knew how to proceed, therefore when the necessity of writing a name in the upper left-hand corner appeared – the sender – she wrote in a bold, desperate hand: 'John Smith, Watertown.'

When this was all done to her satisfaction, she tucked the package under one arm, tried to look as if it weren't heavy, and sauntered downstairs with outward self-possession and inward apprehension. She faced the clerk cordially, while a singularly distracting smile curled her lips.

'My bill, please?' she asked.

'Two dollars, madam,' he responded gallantly.

'I don't happen to have any money with me,' she explained charmingly. 'Of course, I had expected to go back on my wheel, but, since it is broken, perhaps you would be willing to take this until I return to the city and can mail a check?'

She drew a diamond ring from an aristocratic finger and offered it to the clerk. He blushed furiously, and she reproved him for it with a cold stare.

'It's quite irregular,' he explained, 'but, of course, in the circumstances, it will be all right. It is not necessary for us to keep the ring at all, if you will give us your city address.'

'I prefer that you keep it,' she insisted firmly, 'for, besides, I shall have to ask you to let me have fare back to the city – a couple of dollars? Of course it will be all right?'

It was half an hour before the clerk fully awoke. He had given the Girl two real dollars and held her ring clasped firmly in one hand. She was gone. She might just as well have taken the hotel along with her so far as any objection from that clerk would have been concerned.

Once out of the hotel the Girl hurried on.

'Thank goodness, that's over,' she exclaimed.

For several blocks she walked on. Finally her eye was attracted by a 'To Let' sign on a small house – it was No. 410 State Street. She walked in through a gate cut in the solid wall of stone and strolled up to the house. Here she wandered about for a time, incidentally tearing off the 'To Let' sign. Then she came down the path toward the street again. Just inside the stone fence she left her express package, after scribbling the name of the street on it with a pencil. A dollar bill lay on top. She hurried out and along a block or more to a small grocery.

'Will you please phone to the express company and have them send a wagon to No. 410 State Street for a package?' she asked sweetly of a heavy-voiced grocer.

'Certainly, ma'am,' he responded with alacrity.

She paused until he had done as she requested, then dropped into a restaurant for a cup of coffee. She lingered there for a long time, and then went out to spend a greater part of the day wandering up and down State Street. At last an express wagon drove up, the driver went in and returned after a little while with the package.

'And, thank goodness, that's off my hands!' sighed the Girl. 'Now I'm going home.'

Late that evening, Saturday, Miss Dollie Meredith returned to the home of the Greytons and was clasped to the motherly bosom of Mrs Greyton, where she wept unreservedly.

CHAPTER 5

It was late Sunday afternoon. Hutchinson Hatch did not run lightly up the steps of the Greyton home and toss his cigar away as he rang the bell. He did go up the steps, but it was reluctantly, dragging one foot after the other, this being an indication rather of his mental condition than of physical weariness. He did not throw away his cigar as he rang the bell because he wasn't smoking – but he did ring the bell. The maid whom he had seen on his previous visit opened the door.

'Is Mrs Greyton in?' he asked with a nod of recognition.

'No, sir.'

'Mr Greyton?'

'No, sir.'

'Did Mr Meredith arrive from Baltimore?'

'Yes, sir. Last midnight.'

'Ah! Is he in?'

'No, sir.'

The reporter's disappointment showed clearly in his face.

'I don't suppose you've heard anything further from Miss Meredith?' he ventured hopelessly.

'She's upstairs, sir.'

Anyone who has ever stepped on a tack knows just how Hatch felt. He didn't stand on the order of being invited in – he went in. Being in, he extracted a plain calling-card from his pocketbook with twitching fingers and handed it to the waiting maid.

'When did she return?' he asked.

'Last night, about nine, sir.'

'Where has she been?'

'I don't know, sir.'

'Kindly hand her my card and explain to her that it is imperative that I see her for a few minutes,' the reporter went on. 'Impress upon her the absolute necessity of this. By the way, I suppose you know where I came from, eh?'

'Police headquarters, yes, sir.'

Hatch tried to look like a detective, but a gleam of intelligence in his face almost betrayed him.

'You might intimate as much to Miss Meredith,' he instructed the maid calmly.

The maid disappeared. Hatch went in and sat down in the reception-room, and said 'Whew!' several times.

'The gold plate returned to Randolph last night by express,' he mused, 'and she returned also, last night. Now what does that mean?'

After a minute or so the maid reappeared to state that Miss Meredith would see him. Hatch received the message gravely and beckoned mysteriously as he sought for a bill in his pocketbook.

'Do you have any idea where Miss Meredith was?'

'No, sir. She didn't even tell Mrs Greyton or her father.'

'What was her appearance?'

'She seemed very tired, sir, and hungry. She still wore the masked ball costume.'

The bill changed hands and Hatch was left alone again. There was a long wait, then a rustle of skirts, a light step, and Miss Dollie Meredith entered.

She was nervous, it is true, and pallid, but there was a suggestion of defiance as well as determination on her pretty mouth. Hatch stared at her in frank admiration for a moment, then, with an effort, proceeded to business.

'I presume, Miss Meredith,' he said solemnly, 'that the maid informed you of my identity?'

'Yes,' replied Dollie weakly. 'She said you were a detective.'

'Ah!' exclaimed the reporter meaningly, 'then we understand each other. Now, Miss Meredith, will you tell me, please, just where you have been?'

'No.'

The answer was so prompt and so emphatic that Hatch was a little disconcerted. He cleared his throat and started over again.

'Will you inform me, then, in the interest of justice, where you were on the evening of the Randolph ball?' An ominous threat lay behind the words, Hatch hoped she believed.

'I will not.'

'Why did you disappear?'

'I will not tell you.'

Hatch paused to readjust himself. He was going at things backward. When next he spoke his tone had lost the official tang – he talked like a human being.

'May I ask if you happen to know Richard Herbert?'

The pallor of the girl's face was relieved by a delicious sweep of colour.

'I will not tell you,' she answered.

'And if I say that Mr Herbert happens to be a friend of mine?'

'Well, you ought to be ashamed of yourself!'

Two distracting blue eyes were staring him out of countenance; two scarlet lips were drawn tightly together in reproof of a man who boasted such a friendship; two cheeks flamed with indignation that he should have mentioned the name. Hatch floundered for a moment, then cleared his throat and took a fresh start.

'Will you deny that you saw Richard Herbert on the evening of the masked ball?'

'I will not.'

'Will you admit that you saw him?'

'I will not.'

'Do you know that he was wounded?'

'Certainly.'

Now, Hatch had always held a vague theory that the easiest way to make a secret known was to entrust it to a woman. At this point he revised his draw, threw his hand in the pack, and asked for a new deal.

'Miss Meredith,' he said soothingly after a pause, 'will you admit or deny that you ever heard of the Randolph robbery?'

'I will not,' she began, then: 'Certainly I know of it.'

'You know that a man and a woman are accused of and sought for the theft?'

'Yes, I know that.'

'You will admit that you know the man was in Burglar's garb, and that the woman was dressed in a Western costume?'

'The newspapers say that, yes,' she replied sweetly.

'You know, too, that Richard Herbert went to that ball in Burglar's garb and that you went there dressed as a Western girl?' The reporter's tone was strictly professional now.

Dollie stared into the stern face of her interrogator and her courage oozed away. The colour left her face and she wept violently.

'I beg your pardon,' Hatch expostulated. 'I beg your pardon. I didn't mean it just that way, but –'

He stopped helplessly and stared at this wonderful woman with the red hair. Of all things in the world tears were quite the most disconcerting.

'I beg your pardon,' he repeated awkwardly.

Dollie looked up with tear-stained, pleading eyes, then arose and placed both her hands on Hatch's arm. It was a pitiful, helpless sort of a gesture; Hatch shuddered with sheer delight.

'I don't know how you found out about it,' she said tremulously, 'but, if you've come to arrest me, I'm ready to go with you.'

'Arrest you?' gasped the reporter.

'Certainly. I'll go and be locked up. That's what they do, isn't it?' she questioned innocently.

The reporter stared.

'I wouldn't arrest you for a million dollars!' he stammered in dire confusion. 'It wasn't quite that. It was –'

And five minutes later Hutchinson Hatch found himself wandering aimlessly up and down the sidewalk.

CHAPTER 6

Dick Herbert lay stretched lazily on a couch in his room with hands pressed to his eyes. He had just read the Sunday newspapers announcing the mysterious return of the Randolph plate, and naturally he had a headache. Somewhere in a remote recess of his brain mental pyrotechnics were at play; a sort of intellectual pinwheel spouted senseless ideas and suggestions of senseless ideas. The late afternoon shaded off into twilight, twilight into dusk, dusk into darkness, and still he lay motionless.

After a while, from below, he heard the tinkle of a bell and Blair entered with light tread: 'Beg pardon, sir, are you asleep?'

'Who is it, Blair?'

'Mr Hatch, sir.'

'Let him come up.'

Dick arose, snapped on the electric lights, and stood blinkingly in the sudden glare. When Hatch entered they faced each other silently for a moment. There was that in the reporter's eyes that interested Dick immeasurably; there was that in Dick's eyes that Hatch was trying vainly to fathom. Dick relieved a certain vague tension by extending his left hand. Hatch shook it cordially.

'Well?' Dick inquired.

Hatch dropped into a chair and twirled his hat.

'Heard the news?' he asked.

'The return of the gold plate, yes,' and Dick passed a hand across his fevered brow. 'It makes me dizzy.'

'Heard anything from Miss Meredith?'

'No. Why?'

'She returned to the Greytons last night.'

'Returned to the –' and Dick started up suddenly. 'Well, there's no reason why she shouldn't have,' he added. 'Do you happen to know where she was?'

The reporter shook his head.

'I don't know anything,' he said wearily, 'except –' He paused.

Dick paced back and forth across the room several times with one hand pressed to his forehead. Suddenly he turned on his visitor.

'Except what?' he demanded.

'Except that Miss Meredith, by action and word, has convinced me that she either had a hand in the disappearance of the Randolph plate or else knows who was the cause of its disappearance.'

Dick glared at him savagely.

'You know she didn't take the plate?' he demanded.

'Certainly,' replied the reporter. 'That's what makes it all the more astonishing. I talked to her this afternoon, and when I finished she seemed to think I had come to arrest her, and she wanted to go to jail. I nearly fainted.'

Dick glared incredulously, then resumed his nervous pacing. Suddenly he stopped.

'Did she mention my name?'

'I mentioned it. She wouldn't admit even that she knew you.'

There was a pause.

'I don't blame her,' Dick remarked enigmatically. 'She must think me a cad.'

Another pause.

'Well, what about it all, anyhow?' Dick went on finally. 'The plate has been returned, therefore the matter is at an end.'

'Now look here, Dick,' said Hatch. 'I want to say something, and don't go crazy, please, until I finish. I know an awful lot about this affair – things the police never will know. I haven't printed anything much for obvious reasons.'

Dick looked at him apprehensively.

'Go on,' he urged.

'I could print things I know,' the reporter resumed; 'swear out a warrant for you in connection with the gold plate affair and have you arrested and convicted on your own statements, supplemented by those of Miss Meredith. Yet, remember, please, neither your name nor hers has been mentioned as yet.'

Dick took it calmly; he only stared.

'Do you believe that I stole the plate?' he asked.

'Certainly I do not,' replied Hatch, 'but I can prove that you did; prove it to the satisfaction of any jury in the world, and no denial of yours would have any effect.'

'Well?' asked Dick, after a moment.

'Further, I can, on information in my possession, swear out a warrant for Miss Meredith, prove she was in the automobile, and convict her as your accomplice. Now that's a silly state of affairs, isn't it?'

'But, man, you can't believe that she had anything to do with it! She's – she's not that kind.'

'I could take oath that she didn't have anything to do with it, but all the same I can prove that she did,' replied Hatch. 'Now what I am getting at is this: if the police should happen to find out what I know they would send you up – both of you.'

'Well, you are decent about it, old man, and I appreciate it,' said Dick warmly. 'But what can we do?'

'It behoves us – Miss Meredith and you and myself – to get the true facts in the case all together before you get pinched,' said the reporter judicially. 'Suppose now, just suppose, that we three get together and tell each other the truth for a change, the whole truth, and see what will happen?'

'If I should tell you the truth,' said Dick dispassionately, 'it would bring everlasting disgrace on Miss Meredith, and I'd be a beast for doing it; if she told you the truth she would unquestionably send me to prison for theft.'

'But here –' Hatch expostulated.

'Just a minute!' Dick disappeared into another room, leaving the reporter to chew on what he had, then returned in a little while, dressed for the street. 'Now, Hatch,' he said, 'I'm going to try to get to Miss Meredith, but I don't believe she'll see me. If she will, I may be able to explain several things that will clear up this affair in your mind, at any rate. If I don't see her – By the way, did her father arrive from Baltimore?'

'Yes.'

'Good!' exclaimed Dick. 'I'll see him, too – make a show-down of it, and when it's all over I'll let you know what happened.'

Hatch went back to his shop and threatened to kick the office-boy into the wastebasket.

At just about that moment Mr Meredith, in the Greyton home, was reading a card on which appeared the name, 'Mr Richard Hamilton Herbert'. Having read it, he snorted his indignation and went into the reception-room. Dick arose to greet him and offered a hand, which was promptly declined.

'I'd like to ask you, Mr Meredith,' Dick began with a certain steely coldness in his manner, 'just why you object to my attention to your daughter, Dorothy?'

'You know well enough!' raged the old man.

'It is because of the trouble I had in Harvard with your son, Harry. Well and good, but is that all? Is that to stand forever?'

'You proved then that you were not a gentleman,' declared the old man savagely. 'You're a puppy, sir.'

'If you didn't happen to be the father of the girl I'm in love with I'd poke you in the nose,' Dick replied, almost cheerfully. 'Where is your son now? Is there no way I can place myself right in your eyes?'

'No!' Mr Meredith thundered. 'An apology would only be a confession of your dishonour!'

Dick was nearly choking, but managed to keep his voice down.

'Does your daughter know anything of that affair?'

'Certainly not.'

'Where is your son?'

'None of your business, sir!'

'I don't suppose there's any doubt in your mind of my affection for your daughter?'

'I suppose you do admire her,' snapped the old man. 'You can't help that, I suppose. No one can,' he added naively.

'And I suppose you know that she loves me, in spite of your objections?' went on the young man.

'Bah! Bah!'

'And that you are breaking her heart by your mutton-headed objection to me?'

'You – you –' sputtered Mr Meredith.

Dick was still calm.

'May I see Miss Meredith for a few minutes?' he went on.

'She won't see you, sir,' stormed the irate parent. 'She told me last night that she would never consent to see you again.'

'Will you give me your permission to see her here and now, if she will consent?' Dick insisted steadily.

'She won't see you, I say.'

'May I send a card to her?'

'She won't see you, sir,' repeated Mr Meredith doggedly.

Dick stepped out into the hall and beckoned to the maid.

'Please take my card to Miss Meredith,' he directed.

The maid accepted the white square, with a little uplifting of her brows, and went up the stairs. Miss Meredith received it languidly, read it, then sat up indignantly.

'Dick Herbert!' she exclaimed incredulously. 'How dare he come here? It's the most audacious thing I ever heard of! Certainly I will not see him again in any circumstances.' She arose and glared defiantly at the demure maid. 'Tell Mr Herbert,' she said emphatically, 'tell him – that I'll be right down.'

CHAPTER 7

Mr Meredith had stamped out of the room angrily, and Dick Herbert was alone when Dollie, in regal indignation, swept in. The general slant of her ruddy head radiated defiance, and a most depressing chilliness lay in her blue eyes. Her lips formed a scarlet line, and there was a how-dare-you-sir tilt to nose and chin. Dick started up quickly at her appearance.

'Dollie!' he exclaimed eagerly.

'Mr Herbert,' she responded coldly. She sat down primly on the extreme edge of a chair which yawned to embrace her. 'What is it, please?'

Dick was a singularly audacious sort of person, but her manner froze him into sudden austerity. He regarded her steadily for a moment.

'I have come to explain why –'

Miss Dollie Meredith sniffed.

'I have come to explain,' he went on, 'why I did not meet you at the Randolph masked ball, as we had planned.'

'Why you did not meet me?' inquired Dollie coldly, with a little surprised movement of her arched brows. 'Why you did not meet me?' she repeated.

'I shall have to ask you to believe that, in the circumstances, it was absolutely impossible,' Dick continued, preferring not to notice the singular emphasis of her words. 'Something occurred early that evening which – which left me no choice in the matter. I can readily understand your indignation and humiliation at my failure to appear, and I had no way of reaching you that evening or since. News of your return last night only reached me an hour ago. I knew you had disappeared.'

Dollie's blue eyes were opened to the widest and her lips parted a little in astonishment. For a moment she sat thus, staring at the young man, then she sank back into her chair with a little gasp.

'May I inquire,' she asked, after she recovered her breath, 'the cause of this – this levity?'

'Dollie, dear, I am perfectly serious,' Dick assured her earnestly. 'I am trying to make it plain to you, that's all.'

'Why you did not meet me?' Dollie repeated again. 'Why you did meet me! And that's – that's what's the matter with everything!'

Whatever surprise or other emotion Dick might have felt was admirably repressed.

'I thought perhaps there was some mistake somewhere,' he said at last. 'Now, Dollie, listen to me. No, wait a minute, please! I did not go to the Randolph ball. You did. You eloped from that ball, as you and I had planned, in an automobile, but not with me. You went with some other man – the man who really stole the gold plate.'

Dollie opened her mouth to exclaim, then shut it suddenly.

'Now just a moment, please,' pleaded Dick. 'You spoke to some other man under the impression that you were speaking to me. For a reason which does not appear now, he fell in with your plans. Therefore, you ran away with him – in the automobile which carried the gold plate. What happened after that I cannot even surmise. I only know that you are the mysterious woman who disappeared with the Burglar.'

Dollie gasped and nearly choked with her emotions. A flame of scarlet leaped into her face and the glare of the blue eyes was pitiless.

'Mr Herbert,' she said deliberately at last, 'I don't know whether you think I am a fool or only a child. I know that no rational human being can accept that as true. I know I left Seven Oaks with you in the auto; I know you are the man who stole the gold plate; I know how you received the shot in your right shoulder; I know how you afterward fainted from loss of blood. I know how I bound up your wound and – and – I know a lot of things else!'

The sudden rush of words left her breathless for an instant. Dick listened quietly. He started to say something – to expostulate – but she got a fresh start and hurried on: 'I recognised you in that silly disguise by the cleft in your chin. I called you Dick and you answered me. I asked if you had received the little casket and you answered yes. I left the ballroom as you directed and climbed into the automobile. I know that horrid ride we had, and how I took the gold plate in the bag and walked – walked through the night until I was exhausted. I know it all – how I lied and connived, and told silly stories – but I did it all to save you from yourself, and now you dare face me with a denial!'

Dollie suddenly burst into tears. Dick now attempted no further denial. There was no anger in his face – only a deeply troubled expression. He arose and walked over to the window, where he stood staring out.

'I know it all,' Dollie repeated gurglingly – 'all, except what possible idea you had in stealing the miserable, wretched old plate, anyway!' There was a pause and Dollie peered through teary fingers. 'How – how long,' she asked, 'have you been a – a – a – kleptomaniac?'

Dick shrugged his sturdy shoulders a little impatiently.

'Did your father ever happen to tell you why he objects to my attentions to you?' he asked.

'No, but I know now.' And there was a new burst of tears. 'It's because – because you are a – a – you take things.'

'You will not believe what I tell you?'

'How can I when I helped you run away with the horrid stuff?'

'If I pledge you my word of honour that I told you the truth?'

'I can't believe it, I can't!' wailed Dollie desolately. 'No one could believe it. I never suspected – never dreamed – of the possibility of such a thing even when you lay wounded out there in the dark woods. If I had, I should certainly have never – have never – kissed you.'

Dick wheeled suddenly.

'Kissed me?' he exclaimed.

'Yes, you horrid thing!' sobbed Dollie. 'If there had previously been the slightest doubt in my mind as to your identity, that would have convinced me that it was you, because – because – just because! And besides, if it wasn't you I kissed, you ought to have told me!'

Dollie leaned forward suddenly on the arm of the chair with her face hidden in her hands. Dick crossed the room softly toward her and laid a hand caressingly about her shoulders. She shook it off angrily.

'How dare you, sir?' she blazed.

'Dollie, don't you love me?' he pleaded.

'No!' was the prompt reply.

'But you did love me – once?'

'Why – yes, but I – I –'

'And couldn't you ever love me again?'

'I – I don't ever want to again.'

'But couldn't you?'

'If you had only told me the truth, instead of making such a silly denial,' she blubbered. 'I don't know why you took the plate unless – unless it is because you – you couldn't help it. But you didn't tell me the truth.'

Dick stared down at the ruddy head moodily for a moment. Then his manner changed and he dropped on his knees beside her.

'Suppose,' he whispered, 'suppose I should confess that I did take it?'

Dollie looked up suddenly with a new horror in her face.

'Oh, you did do it then?' she demanded. This was worse than ever!

'Suppose I should confess that I did?'

'Oh, Dick!' she sobbed. And her arms went suddenly around his neck. 'You are breaking my heart. Why? Why?'

'Would you be satisfied?' he insisted.

'What could have caused you to do such a thing?'

The love-light glimmered again in her blue eyes; the red lips trembled.

'Suppose it had been just a freak of mine, and I had intended to – to return the stuff, as has been done?' he went on.

Dollie stared deeply into the eyes upturned to hers.

'Silly boy,' she said. Then she kissed him. 'But you must never, never do it again.'

'I never will,' he promised solemnly.

Five minutes later Dick was leaving the house, when he met Mr Meredith in the hall.

'I'm going to marry your daughter,' he said quite calmly.

Mr Meredith raved at him as he went down the steps.

CHAPTER 8

Alone in her room, with the key turned in the lock, Miss Dollie Meredith had a perfectly delightful time. She wept and laughed and sobbed and shuddered; she was pensive and doleful and happy and melancholy; she dreamed dreams of the future, past and present; she sang foolish little ecstatic songs – just a few words of each – and cried again copiously. Her father had sent her to her room with a stern reprimand, and she giggled joyously as she remembered it.

'After all, it wasn't anything,' she assured herself. 'It was silly for him to – to take the stuff, of course, but it's back now, and he told me the truth, and he intended to return it, anyway.' In her present mood she would have justified anything. 'And he's not a thief or anything. I don't suppose father will ever give his consent, so, after all, we'll have to elope, and that will be – perfectly delightful. Papa will go on dreadfully and then he'll be all right.'

After a while Dollie snuggled down in the sheets and lay quite still in the dark until sleep overtook her. Silence reigned in the house. It was about two o'clock in the morning when she sat up suddenly in bed with startled eyes. She had heard something – or rather in her sleep she had received the impression of hearing something. She listened intently as she peered about.

Finally she did hear something – something tap sharply on the window once. Then came silence again. A frightened chill ran all the way down to Dollie's curling pink toes. There was a pause, and then again came the sharp click on the window, whereupon Dollie pattered out of bed in her bare feet and ran to the window, which was open a few inches.

With the greatest caution she peered out. Vaguely skulking in the shadows below she made out the figure of a man. As she looked it seemed to draw up into a knot, then straighten out quickly. Involuntarily she dodged. There came another sharp click at the window. The man below was tossing pebbles against the pane with the obvious purpose of attracting her attention.

'Dick, is that you?' she called cautiously.

'Sh – h – h – h!' came the answer. 'Here's a note for you. Open the window so I may throw it in.'

'Is it really and truly you?' Dollie insisted.

'Yes,' came the hurried, whispered answer. 'Quick, someone is coming!'

Dollie threw the sash up and stepped back. A whirling, white object came through and fell noiselessly on the carpet. Dollie seized upon it eagerly and ran to the window again. Below she saw the retreating figure of a man. Other footsteps materialised in a bulky policeman, who strolled by seeking, perhaps, a quiet spot for a nap.

Shivering with excitement, Dollie closed the window and pulled down the shade, after which she lighted the gas. She opened the note eagerly and sat down upon the floor to read it. Now a large part of this note was extraneous verbiage of a superlative emotional nature – its vital importance was an outline of a new plan of elopement, to take place on Wednesday in time for them to catch a European-bound steamer at half-past two in the afternoon.

Dollie read and reread the crumpled sheet many times, and when finally its wording had been indelibly fixed in her mind she wasted an unbelievable number of kisses on it. Of course this was sheer extravagance, but – girls are wonderful creatures.

'He's the dearest thing in the world!' she declared at last.

She burned the note reluctantly and carefully disposed of the ashes by throwing them out of the window, after which she returned to her bed. On the following morning, Monday, father glared at daughter sternly as she demurely entered the breakfast-room. He was seeking to read that which no man has ever been able to read – a woman's face. Dollie smiled upon him charmingly.

After breakfast father and daughter had a little talk in a sunny corner of the library.

'I have planned for us to return to Baltimore on next Thursday,' he informed her.

'Oh, isn't that delightful?' beamed Dollie.

'In view of everything and your broken promise to me – the promise not to see Herbert again – I think it wisest,' he continued.

'Perhaps it is,' she mused.

'Why did you see him?' he demanded.

'I consented to see him, only to bid him goodbye,' replied Dollie demurely, 'and to make perfectly clear to him my position in this matter.'

Oh, woman! Perfidious, insincere, loyal, charming woman! All the tangled skeins of life are the work of your dainty fingers. All the sins and sorrows are your doing!

Mr Meredith rubbed his chin thoughtfully.

'You may take it as my wish – my order even,' he said as he cleared his throat – for giving orders to Dollie was a dangerous experiment, 'that you must not attempt to communicate in any way with Mr Herbert again – by letter or otherwise.'

'Yes, papa.'

Mr Meredith was somewhat surprised at the ease with which he got away with this. Had he been blessed with a little more wisdom in the ways of women he would have been suspicious.

'You really do not love him, anyway,' he ventured at last. 'It was only a girlish infatuation.'

'I told him yesterday just what I thought of him,' she replied truthfully enough.

And thus the interview ended.

It was about noon that day when Hutchinson Hatch called on Dick Herbert.

'Well, what did you find out?' he inquired.

'Really, old man,' said Dick kindly, 'I have decided that there is nothing I can say to you about the matter. It's a private affair, after all.'

'Yes, I know that you know about that, but the police don't know it,' commented the reporter grimly.

'The police!' Dick smiled.

'Did you see her?' Hatch asked.

'Yes, I saw her – and her father, too.'

Hatch saw the one door by which he had hoped to solve the riddle closing on him.

'Was Miss Meredith the girl in the automobile?' he asked bluntly.

'Really, I won't answer that.'

'Are you the man who stole the gold plate?'

'I won't answer that, either,' replied Dick smilingly. 'Now, look here, Hatch, you're a good fellow. I like you. It is your business to find out things, but, in this particular affair, I'm going to make it my business to keep you from finding out things. I'll risk the police end of it.' He went over and shook hands with the reporter cordially. 'Believe me, if I told you the absolute truth – all of it – you couldn't print it unless – unless I was arrested, and I don't intend that that shall happen.'

Hatch went away.

That night the Randolph gold plate was stolen for the second time. Thirty-six hours later Detective Mallory arrested Richard Herbert with the stolen plate in his possession. Dick burst out laughing when the detective walked in on him.

Part 3:
The Thinking Machine

CHAPTER 1

Professor Augustus S. F. X. Van Dusen, Ph.D., LL.D., F.R.S., M.D., etc., etc., was the Court of Last Appeal in the sciences. He was five feet two inches tall, weighed 107 pounds, that being slightly above normal, and wore a number eight hat. Bushy, yellow hair straggled down about his ears and partially framed a clean-shaven, wizened face in which were combined the paradoxical qualities of extreme aggressiveness and childish petulance. The mouth drooped a little at the corners, being otherwise a straight line; the eyes were mere slits of blue, squinting eternally through thick spectacles. His brow rose straight up, domelike, majestic even, and added a whimsical grotesqueness to his appearance.

The Professor's idea of light literature, for rare moments of recreation, was page after page of encyclopaedic discussion on 'ologies' and 'isms' with lots of figures in 'em. Sometimes he wrote these discussions himself, and frequently held them up to annihilation. His usual speaking tone was one of deep annoyance, and he had an unwavering glare that went straight through one. He was the son of the son of the son of an eminent German scientist, the logical production of a house that had borne a distinguished name in the sciences for generations.

Thirty-five of his fifty years had been devoted to logic, study, analysis of cause and effect, mental, material and psychological. By his personal efforts he had mercilessly flattened out and readjusted at least two of the exact sciences and had added immeasurably to the world's sum of knowledge in others. Once he had held the chair of philosophy in a great university, but casually one day he promulgated a thesis that knocked the faculty's eye out, and he was invited to vacate. It was a dozen years later that that university had openly resorted to influence and diplomacy to induce him to accept its LL.D.

For years foreign and American institutions, educational, scientific and otherwise, crowded degrees upon him. He didn't care. He started fires with the elaborately formal notifications of these unsought honours and turned again to his work in the small laboratory which was a part of his modest home. There he lived, practically a recluse, his simple wants being attended to by one aged servant, Martha.

This, then, was The Thinking Machine. This last title, The Thinking Machine, perhaps more expressive of the real man than a yard of honorary initials, was coined by Hutchinson Hatch at the time of the scientist's defeat of a chess champion after a single morning's instruction in the game. The Thinking Machine had asserted that logic was inevitable, and that game had proven his assertion. Afterward there had grown up a strange sort of friendship between the crabbed scientist and the reporter. Hatch, to the scientist, represented the great, whirling outside world; to the reporter the scientist was merely a brain – a marvellously keen, penetrating, infallible guide through material muddles far removed from the delicately precise labours of the laboratory.

Now The Thinking Machine sat in a huge chair in his reception-room with long, slender fingers pressed tip to tip and squint eyes turned upward. Hatch was talking, had been talking for more than an hour with infrequent interruptions. In that time he had laid bare the facts as he and the police knew them from the incidents of the masked ball at Seven Oaks to the return of Dollie Meredith.

'Now, Mr Hatch,' asked The Thinking Machine, 'just what is known of this second theft of the gold plate?'

'It's simple enough,' explained the reporter. 'It was plain burglary. Some person entered the Randolph house on Monday night by cutting out a pane of glass and unfastening a window-latch. Whoever it was took the plate and escaped. That's all anyone knows of it.'

'Left no clue, of course?'

'No, so far as has been found.'

'I presume that, on its return by express, Mr Randolph ordered the plate placed in the small room as before?'

'Yes.'

'He's a fool.'

'Yes.'

'Please go on.'

'Now the police absolutely decline to say as yet just what evidence they have against Herbert beyond the finding of the plate in his possession,' the reporter resumed, 'though, of course, that's enough and to spare. They will not say, either, how they first came to connect him with the affair. Detective Mallory doesn't –'

'When and where was Mr Herbert arrested?'

'Yesterday, Tuesday, afternoon in his rooms. Fourteen pieces of the gold plate were on the table.'

The Thinking Machine dropped his eyes a moment to squint at the reporter.

'Only eleven pieces of the plate were first stolen, you said?'

'Only eleven, yes.'

'And I think you said two shots were fired at the thief?'

'Yes.'

'Who fired them, please?'

'One of the detectives – Cunningham, I think.'

'It was a detective – you know that?'

'Yes, I know that.'

'Yes, yes. Please go on.'

'The plate was all spread out – there was no attempt to conceal it,' Hatch resumed. 'There was a box on the floor and Herbert was about to pack the stuff in it when Detective Mallory and two of his men entered. Herbert's servant, Blair, was away from the house at the time. His people are up in Nova Scotia, so he was alone.'

'Nothing but the gold plate was found?'

'Oh, yes!' exclaimed the reporter. 'There was a lot of jewelry in a case and fifteen or twenty odd pieces – $50,000 worth of stuff, at least. The police took it to find the owners.'

'Dear me! Dear me!' exclaimed The Thinking Machine. 'Why didn't you mention the jewelry at first? Wait a minute.'

Hatch was silent while the scientist continued to squint at the ceiling. He wriggled in his chair uncomfortably and smoked a couple of cigarettes before The Thinking Machine turned to him and nodded.

'That's all I know,' said Hatch.

'Did Mr Herbert say anything when arrested?'

'No, he only laughed. I don't know why. I don't imagine it would have been at all funny to me.'

'Has he said anything since?'

'No, nothing to me or anybody else. He was arraigned at a preliminary hearing, pleaded not guilty, and was released on $20,000 bail. Some of his rich friends furnished it.'

'Did he give any reason for his refusal to say anything?' insisted The Thinking Machine testily.

'He remarked to me that he wouldn't say anything, because, even if he told the truth, no one would believe him.'

'If it should have been a protestation of innocence I'm afraid nobody would have believed him,' commented the scientist enigmatically. He was silent for several minutes. 'It could have been a brother, of course,' he mused.

'A brother?' asked Hatch quickly. 'Whose brother? What brother?'

'As I understand it,' the scientist went on, not heeding the question, 'you did not believe Herbert guilty of the first theft?'

'Why, I couldn't,' Hatch protested. 'I couldn't,' he repeated. 'Why?'

'Well, because – because he's not that sort of man,' explained the reporter. 'I've known him for years, personally and by reputation.'

'Was he a particular friend of yours in college?'

'No, not an intimate, but he was in my class – and he's a whacking, jam-up, ace-high football player.' That squared everything.

'Do you now believe him guilty?' insisted the scientist.

'I can't believe anything else – and yet I'd stake my life on his honesty.'

'And Miss Meredith?'

The reporter was reaching the explosive point. He had seen and talked to Miss Meredith, you know.

'It's perfectly asinine to suppose that she had anything to do with either theft, don't you think?'

The Thinking Machine was silent on that point.

'Well, Mr Hatch,' he said finally, 'the problem comes down to this: did a man, and perhaps a woman, who are circumstantially proven guilty of stealing the gold plate, actually steal it? We have the stained cushion of the automobile in which the thieves escaped to indicate that one of them was wounded; we have Mr Herbert with an injured right shoulder – a hurt received that night on his own statement, though he won't say how. We have, then, the second theft and the finding of the stolen property in his possession along with another lot of stolen stuff – jewels. It is apparently a settled case now without going further.'

'But –' Hatch started to protest.

'But suppose we do go a little further,' The Thinking Machine went on. 'I can prove definitely, conclusively, and finally by settling only two points whether or not Mr Herbert was wounded while in the automobile. If he was wounded while in that automobile, he was the first thief; if not, he wasn't. If he was the first thief, he was probably the second, but even if he were not the first thief, there is, of course, a possibility that he was the second.'

Hatch was listening with mouth open.

'Suppose we begin now,' continued The Thinking Machine, 'by finding out the name of the physician who treated Mr Herbert's wound last Thursday night. Mr Herbert may have a reason for keeping the identity of this physician secret, but, perhaps – wait a minute,' and the scientist disappeared into the next room. He was gone for five minutes. 'See if the physician who treated the wound wasn't Dr Clarence Walpole.'

The reporter blinked a little.

'Right,' he said. 'What next?'

'Ask him something about the nature of the wound and all the usual questions.'

Hatch nodded.

'Then,' resumed The Thinking Machine casually, 'bring me some of Mr Herbert's blood.'

The reporter blinked a good deal, and gulped twice.

'How much?' he inquired briskly.

'A single drop on a small piece of glass will do very nicely,' replied the scientist.

CHAPTER 2

The Supreme Police Intelligence of the Metropolitan District was doing some heavy thinking, which, modestly enough, bore generally on his own dazzling perspicacity. Just at the moment he couldn't recall any detector of crime whose lustre in any way dimmed his own, or whose mere shadow, even, had a right to fall on the same earth as his; and this lapse of memory so stimulated his admiration for the subject of his thoughts that he lighted a fresh cigar and put his feet in the middle of the desk.

He sat thus when The Thinking Machine called. The Supreme Intelligence – Mr Mallory – knew Professor Van Dusen well, and, though he received his visitor graciously, he showed no difficulty in restraining any undue outburst of enthusiasm. Instead, the same admirable self-control which prevented him from outwardly evidencing his pleasure prompted him to square back in his chair with a touch of patronising aggressiveness in his manner.

'Ah, Professor,' was his noncommittal greeting.

'Good evening, Mr Mallory,' responded the scientist in the thin, irritated voice which always set Mr Mallory's nerves a-jangle. 'I don't suppose you would tell me by what steps you were led to arrest Mr Herbert?'

'I would not,' declared Mr Mallory promptly.

'No, nor would you inform me of the nature of the evidence against him in addition to the jewels and plate found in his possession?'

'I would not,' replied Mr Mallory again.

'No, I thought perhaps you would not,' remarked The Thinking Machine. 'I understand, by the way, that one of your men took a leather cushion from the automobile in which the thieves escaped on the night of the ball?'

'Well, what of it?' demanded the detective.

'I merely wanted to inquire if it would be permissible for me to see that cushion?'

Detective Mallory glared at him suspiciously, then slowly his heavy face relaxed, and he laughed as he arose and produced the cushion.

'If you're trying to make any mystery of this cushion, you're in bad,' he informed the scientist. 'We know the owner of the automobile in which Herbert and the Girl escaped. The cushion means nothing.'

The Thinking Machine examined the heavy leather carefully and paid a great deal of attention to the crusted stains which it bore. He picked at one of the brown spots with his penknife and it flaked off in his hand.

'Herbert was caught with the goods on him,' declared the detective, and he thumped the desk with his lusty fist. 'We've got the right man.'

'Yes,' admitted The Thinking Machine, 'it begins to look very much as if you did have the right man – for once.'

Detective Mallory snorted.

'Would you mind telling me if any of the jewelry you found in Mr Herbert's possession has been identified?'

'Sure thing,' replied the detective. 'That's where I've got Herbert good. Four people who lost jewelry at the masked ball have appeared and claimed pieces of the stuff.'

For an instant a slightly perplexed wrinkle appeared in the brow of The Thinking Machine, and as quickly it passed.

'Of course, of course,' he mused.

'It's the biggest haul of stolen goods the police of this city have made for many years,' the detective volunteered complacently. 'And, if I'm not wrong, there's more of it coming – no man knows how much more. Why, Herbert must have been operating for years, and he got away with it, of course, by the gentlemanly exterior, the polish, and all that. I consider his capture the most important that has happened since I have been connected with the police.'

'Indeed?' inquired the scientist thoughtfully. He was still gazing at the cushion.

'And the most important development of all is to come,' Detective Mallory rattled on. 'That will be the real sensation, and make the arrest of Herbert seem purely incidental. It now looks as if there will be another arrest of a – of a person who is so high socially, and all that –'

'Yes,' interrupted The Thinking Machine, 'but do you think it would be wise to arrest her now?'

'Her?' demanded Detective Mallory. 'What do you know of any woman?'

'You were speaking of Miss Dorothy Meredith, weren't you?' inquired The Thinking Machine blandly. 'Well, I merely asked if you thought it would be wise for your men to go so far as to arrest her.'

The detective bit his cigar in two in obvious perturbation.

'How – how – did you happen to know her name?' he demanded.

'Oh, Mr Hatch mentioned it to me,' replied the scientist. 'He has known of her connection with the case for several days, as well as Herbert's, and has talked to them both, I think.'

The Supreme Intelligence was nearly apoplectic.

'If Hatch knew it why didn't he tell me?' he thundered.

'Really, I don't know,' responded the scientist. 'Perhaps,' he added curtly, 'he may have had some absurd notion that you would find it out for yourself. He has strange ideas like that sometimes.'

And when Detective Mallory· had fully recovered The Thinking Machine was gone.

Meanwhile Hatch had seen and questioned Dr Clarence Walpole in the latter's office, only a stone's throw from Dick Herbert's home. Had Doctor Walpole recently dressed a wound for Mr Herbert? Doctor Walpole had. A wound caused by a pistol-bullet? Yes.

'When was it, please?' asked Hatch.

'Only a few nights ago.'

'Thursday night, perhaps?'

Doctor Walpole consulted a desk-diary.

'Yes, Thursday night, or rather Friday morning,' he replied. 'It was between two and three o'clock. He came here and I fixed him up.'

'Where was the wound, please?'

'In the right shoulder,' replied the physician, 'just here,' and he touched the reporter with one finger. 'It wasn't dangerous, but he had lost considerable blood.'

Hatch was silent for a moment, dazed. Every new point piled up the evidence against Herbert. The location of the wound – a pistol-wound – the very hour of the dressing of it! Dick would have had plenty of time between the moment of the robbery, which was comparatively early, and the hour of his call on Doctor Walpole to do all those things which he was suspected of doing.

'I don't suppose Mr Herbert explained how he got the wound?' Hatch asked apprehensively. He was afraid he had.

'No. I asked, but he evaded the question. It was, of course, none of my business, after I had extracted the bullet and dressed the hurt.'

'You have the bullet?'

'Yes. It's the usual size – thirty-two calibre.'

That was all. The prosecution was in, the case proven, the verdict rendered. Ten minutes later Hatch's name was announced to Dick Herbert. Dick received him gloomily, shook hands with him, then resumed his interrupted pacing.

'I had declined to see men from other papers,' he said wearily.

'Now, look here, Dick,' expostulated Hatch, 'don't you want to make some statement of your connection with this affair? I honestly believe that if you did it would help you.'

'No, I cannot make any statement – that's all.' Dick's hand closed fiercely. 'I can't,' he added, 'and there's no need to talk of it.' He continued his pacing for a moment or so; then turned on the reporter. 'Do you believe me guilty?' he demanded abruptly.

'I can't believe anything else,' Hatch replied falteringly. 'But at that I don't want to believe it.' There was an embarrassed pause. 'I have just seen Dr Clarence Walpole.'

'Well?' Dick wheeled on him angrily.

'What he said alone would convict you, even if the stuff had not been found here,' Hatch replied.

'Are you trying to convict me?' Dick demanded.

'I'm trying to get the truth,' remarked Hatch.

'There is just one man in the world whom I must see before the truth can ever be told,' declared Dick vehemently. 'And I can't find him now. I don't know where he is!'

'Let me find him. Who is he? What's his name?'

'If I told you that I might as well tell you everything,' Dick went on. 'It was to prevent any mention of that name that I have allowed myself to be placed in this position. It is purely a personal matter between us – at least I will make it so – and if I ever meet him –' his hands closed and unclosed spasmodically, 'the truth will be known unless I – I kill him first.'

More bewildered, more befuddled, and more generally betangled than ever, Hatch put his hands to his head to keep it from flying off. Finally he glanced around at Dick, who stood with clenched fists and closed teeth. A blaze of madness lay in Dick's eyes.

'Have you seen Miss Meredith again?' inquired the reporter.

Dick burst out laughing.

Half an hour later Hatch left him. On the glass top of an inkstand he carried three precious drops of Herbert's blood.

CHAPTER 3

Faithfully, phonographically even, Hatch repeated to The Thinking Machine the conversation he had had with Doctor Walpole, indicating on the person of the eminent scientist the exact spot of the wound as Doctor Walpole had indicated it to him. The scientist listened without comment to the recital, casually studying meanwhile the three crimson drops on the glass.

'Every step I take forward is a step backward,' the reporter declared in conclusion with a helpless grin. 'Instead of showing that Dick Herbert might not have stolen the plate I am proving conclusively that he was the thief – nailing it to him so hard that he can't possibly get out of it.' He was silent a moment. 'If I keep on long enough,' he added glumly, 'I'll hang him.'

The Thinking Machine squinted at him aggressively.

'You still don't believe him guilty?' he asked.

'Why, I – I – I –' Hatch burst out savagely. 'Damn it, I don't know what I believe,' he tapered off. 'It's absolutely impossible!'

'Nothing is impossible, Mr Hatch,' snapped The Thinking Machine irritably. 'The worst a problem can be is difficult, but all problems can be solved as inevitably as that two and two make four – not sometimes, but all the time. Please don't say things are impossible. It annoys me exceedingly.'

Hatch stared at his distinguished friend and smiled whimsically. He was also annoyed exceedingly on his own private, individual account – the annoyance that comes from irresistibly butting into immovable facts.

'Doctor Walpole's statement,' The Thinking Machine went on after a moment, 'makes this particular problem ludicrously simple. Two points alone show conclusively that Mr Herbert was not the man in the automobile. I shall reach the third myself.'

Hatch didn't say anything. The English language is singularly inadequate at times, and if he had spoken he would have had to invent a phraseology to convey even a faint glimmer of what he really thought.

'Now, Mr Hatch,' resumed the scientist, quite casually, 'I understand you graduated from Harvard in ninety-eight. Yes? Well, Herbert was a classmate of yours there. Please obtain for me one of the printed lists of students who were in Harvard that year – a complete list.'

'I have one at home,' said the reporter.

'Get it, please, immediately, and return here,' instructed the scientist.

Hatch went out and The Thinking Machine disappeared into his laboratory. He remained there for one hour and forty-seven minutes by the clock. When he came out he found the reporter sitting in the reception-room again, holding his head. The scientist's face was as blankly inscrutable as ever.

'Here is the list,' said Hatch as he handed it over.

The Thinking Machine took it in his long, slender fingers and turned two or three leaves. Finally he stopped and ran a finger down one page.

'Ah,' he exclaimed at last. 'I thought so.'

'Thought what?' asked Hatch curiously.

'I'm going out to see Mr Meredith now,' remarked The Thinking Machine irrelevantly. 'Come along. Have you met him?'

'No.'

Mr Meredith had read the newspaper accounts of the arrest of Dick Herbert and the seizure of the gold plate and jewels;

he had even taunted his charming daughter with it in a fatherly sort of a way. She was weeping, weeping her heart out over this latest proof of the perfidy and loathsomeness of the man she loved.

Incidentally, it may be mentioned here that the astute Mr Meredith was not aware of any elopement plot – either the first or second.

When a card bearing the name of Mr Augustus S. F. X. Van Dusen was handed to Mr Meredith he went wonderingly into the reception-room. There was a pause as the scientist and Mr Meredith mentally sized each other up; then introductions – and The Thinking Machine came down to business abruptly, as always.

'May I ask, Mr Meredith,' he began, 'how many sons you have?'

'One,' replied Mr Meredith, puzzled.

'May I ask his present address?' went on the scientist.

Mr Meredith studied the belligerent eyes of his caller and wondered what business it was of his, for Mr Meredith was a belligerent sort of a person himself.

'May I ask,' he inquired with pronounced emphasis on the personal pronoun, 'why you want to know?'

Hatch rubbed his chin thoughtfully. He was wondering what would happen to him when the cyclone struck.

'It may save him and you a great deal of annoyance if you will give me his address,' said The Thinking Machine. 'I desire to communicate with him immediately on a matter of the utmost importance – a purely personal matter.'

'Personal matter?' repeated Mr Meredith. 'Your abruptness and manner, sir, were not calculated to invite confidence.'

The Thinking Machine bowed gravely.

'May I ask your son's address?' he repeated.

Mr Meredith considered the matter at some length and finally arrived at the conclusion that he might ask.

'He is in South America at present – Buenos Aires,' he replied.

'What?' exclaimed The Thinking Machine so suddenly that both Hatch and Mr Meredith started a little. 'What?' he repeated, and wrinkles suddenly appeared in the domelike brow.

'I said he was in South America – Buenos Aires,' repeated Mr Meredith stiffly, but a little awed. 'A letter or cable to him in care of the American Consul at Buenos Aires will reach him promptly.'

The Thinking Machine's narrow eyes were screwed down to the disappearing point, the slender white fingers were twiddled jerkily, the corrugations remained in his brow.

'How long has Mr Meredith been there?' he asked at last.

'Three months.'

'Do you know he is there?'

Mr Meredith started to say something then swallowed it with an effort.

'I know it positively, yes,' he replied. 'I received this letter dated the second from him three days ago, and today I received a cable-dispatch forwarded to me here from Baltimore.'

'Are you positive the letter is in your son's handwriting?'

Mr Meredith almost choked in mingled bewilderment and resentment at the question and the manner of its asking.

'I am positive, yes,' he replied at last, preserving his tone of dignity with a perceptible effort. He noted the inscrutable face of his caller and saw the corrugations in the brow suddenly swept away. 'What business of yours is it, anyway?' blazed Mr Meredith suddenly.

'May I ask where you were last Thursday night?' went on the even, steady voice.

'It's no business of yours,' Mr Meredith blurted. 'I was in Baltimore.'

'Can you prove it in a court of law?'

'Prove it? Of course I can prove it!' Mr Meredith was fairly bellowing at his impassive interrogator. 'But it's nobody's business.'

'If you can prove it, Mr Meredith,' remarked The Thinking Machine quietly, coldly, 'you had best make your arrangements to do so, because, believe me, it may be necessary to save you from a charge of having stolen the Randolph gold plate on last Thursday night at the masked ball. Good-day, sir.'

CHAPTER 4

'But Mr Herbert won't see anyone, sir,' protested Blair.

'Tell Mr Herbert, please, that unless I can see him immediately his bail-bond will be withdrawn,' directed The Thinking Machine.

He stood waiting in the hall while Blair went up the stairs. Dick Herbert took the card impatiently and glanced at it.

'Van Dusen,' he mused. 'Who the deuce is Van Dusen?'

Blair repeated the message he had received below.

'What does he look like?' inquired Dick.

'He's a shrivelled little man with a big yellow head, sir,' replied Blair.

'Let him come up,' instructed Dick.

Thus, within an hour after he had talked to Mr Meredith, The Thinking Machine met Dick Herbert.

'What's this about the bail-bond?' Dick inquired.

'I wanted to talk to you,' was the scientist's calm reply. 'That seemed to be the easiest way to make you believe it was important, so –'

Dick's face flushed crimson at the trick.

'Well, you see me!' he broke out angrily. 'I ought to throw you down the stairs, but – what is it?'

Not having been invited to a seat, The Thinking Machine took one anyway and settled himself comfortably.

'If you will listen to me for a moment without interruption,' he began testily, 'I think the subject of my remarks will be of deep personal concern to you. I am interested in solving this Randolph plate affair and have perhaps gone further in my investigation than anyone else. At least, I know more about it. There are some things I don't happen to know, however, that are of the greatest importance.'

'I tell you –' stormed Dick.

'For instance,' calmly resumed the scientist, 'it is very important for me to know whether or not Harry Meredith was masked when he came into this room last Thursday night.'

Dick gazed at him in surprise which approached awe. His eyes were widely distended, the lower part of his face lax, for the instant; then his white teeth closed with a snap and he sat down opposite The Thinking Machine. Anger had gone from his manner; instead there was a pallor of apprehension in the clean-cut face.

'Who are you, Mr Van Dusen?' he asked at last. His tone was mild, even deferential.

'Was he masked?' insisted the scientist.

For a long while Dick was silent. Finally he arose and paced nervously back and forth across the room, glancing at the diminutive figure of The Thinking Machine each time as he turned.

'I won't say anything,' he decided.

'Will you name the cause of the trouble you and Meredith had at Harvard?' asked the scientist.

Again there was a long pause.

'No,' Dick said finally.

'Did it have anything to do with theft?'

'I don't know who you are or why you are prying into an affair that, at least on its face, does not concern you,' replied Dick. 'I'll say nothing at all – unless – unless you produce the one man who can and shall explain this affair. Produce him here in this room where I can get my hands on him!'

The Thinking Machine squinted at the sturdy shoulders with admiration in his face.

'Did it ever happen to occur to you, Mr Herbert, that Harry Meredith and his father are precisely of the same build?'

Some nameless, impalpable expression crept into Dick's face despite an apparent fight to restrain it, and again he stared at the small man in the chair.

'And that you and Mr Meredith are practically of the same build?'

Tormented by unasked questions and by those emotions which had compelled him to silence all along, Dick still paced back and forth. His head was whirling. The structure which he had so carefully guarded was tumbling about his ears. Suddenly he stopped and turned upon The Thinking Machine.

'Just what do you know of this affair?' he asked.

'I know for one thing,' replied the scientist positively, 'that you were not the man in the automobile.'

'How do you know that?'

'That's beside the question just now.'

'Do you know who was in the automobile?' Dick insisted.

'I can only answer that question when you have answered mine,' the scientist went on. 'Was Harry Meredith masked when he entered this room last Thursday night?'

Dick sat staring down at his hands, which were working nervously. Finally he nodded.

The Thinking Machine understood.

'You recognised him, then, by something he said or wore?'

Again Dick nodded reluctantly.

'Both,' he added.

The Thinking Machine leaned back in his chair and sat there for a long time. At last he arose as if the interview were at an end. There seemed to be no other questions that he desired to ask at the moment.

'You need not be unnecessarily alarmed, Mr Herbert,' he assured Dick as he picked up his hat. 'I shall act with discretion in this matter. I am not representing anyone who would care to make it unpleasant for you. I may tell you that you made two serious mistakes: the first when you saw or communicated with Mr Randolph immediately after the plate was stolen the second time, and again when you undertook something which properly belonged within the province of the police.'

Herbert still sat with his head in his hands as The Thinking Machine went out.

It was very late that night – after twelve, in fact – when Hutchinson Hatch called on The Thinking Machine with excitement evident in tone, manner and act. He was accustomed to calling at any hour; now he found the scientist at work as if it were midday.

'The worst has happened,' the reporter told him.

The Thinking Machine didn't look around.

'Detective Mallory and two of his men saw Miss Meredith this evening about nine o'clock,' Hatch hurried on, 'and bully-ragged her into a confession.'

'What sort of a confession?'

'She admitted that she was in the automobile on the night of the ball and that –'

'Mr Herbert was with her,' the scientist supplied.

'Yes.'

'And – what else?'

'That her own jewels, valued at $20,000, were among those found in Herbert's possession when he was arrested.'

The Thinking Machine turned and looked at the reporter, just casually, and raised his hand to his mouth to cover a yawn.

'Well, she couldn't do anything else,' he said calmly.

CHAPTER 5

Hutchinson Hatch remained with The Thinking Machine for more than an hour, and when he left his head was spinning with the multitude of instructions which had been heaped upon him.

'Meet me at noon in Detective Mallory's office at police headquarters,' The Thinking Machine had said in conclusion. 'Mr Randolph and Miss Meredith will be there.'

'Miss Meredith?' Hatch repeated. 'She hasn't been arrested, you know, and I doubt if she will come.'

'She will come,' the scientist had replied, as if that settled it.

Next day the Supreme Intelligence was sitting in his private office. He had eaten the canary; mingled triumph and gratification beamed upon his countenance. The smile remained, but to it was added the quality of curiosity when the door opened and The Thinking Machine, accompanied by Dollie Meredith and Stuyvesant Randolph, entered.

'Mr Hatch called yet?' inquired the scientist.

'No,' responded the detective.

'Dear me!' grumbled the other. 'It's one minute after twelve o'clock now. What could have delayed him?'

His answer was the clattering rush of a cab and the appearance of Hatch in person a moment later. He came into the room headlong, glanced around, then paused.

'Did you get it?' inquired The Thinking Machine.

'Yes, I got it, but –' began the reporter.

'Nothing else now,' commanded the other.

There was a little pause as The Thinking Machine selected a chair. The others also sat down.

'Well?' inquired the Supreme Intelligence at last.

'I would like to ask, Mr Mallory,' the scientist said, 'if it would be possible for me to convince you of Mr Herbert's innocence of the charges against him?'

'It would not,' replied the detective promptly. 'It would not while the facts are before me, supplemented by the statement of Miss Meredith here – her confession.'

Dollie coloured exquisitely and her lips trembled slightly.

'Would it be possible, Miss Meredith,' the even voice went on, 'to convince you of Mr Herbert's innocence?'

'I – I don't think so,' she faltered. 'I – I know.'

Tears which had been restrained with difficulty gushed forth suddenly, and The Thinking Machine squinted at her in pained surprise.

'Don't do that,' he commanded. 'It's – it's exceedingly irritating.' He paused a moment, then turned suddenly to Mr Randolph. 'And you?' he asked.

Mr Randolph shrugged his shoulders.

The Thinking Machine receded still further into his chair and stared dreamily upward with his long, slender fingers pressed tip to tip. Hatch knew the attitude; something was going to happen. He waited anxiously. Detective Mallory knew it, too, and wriggled uncomfortably.

'Suppose,' the scientist began, 'just suppose that we turn a little human intelligence on this problem for a change and see if we can't get the truth out of the blundering muddle that the police have helped to bring about. Let's use logic, inevitable logic, to show, simply enough, that instead of being guilty, Mr Herbert is innocent.'

Dolly Meredith suddenly leaned forward in her chair with flushed face, eyes widely opened and lips slightly parted. Detective Mallory also leaned forward in his chair, but there was a different expression on his face – oh, so different.

'Miss Meredith, we know you were in the automobile with the Burglar who stole the plate,' The Thinking Machine went on. 'You probably knew that he was wounded and possibly either aided in dressing the wound – as any woman would – or else saw him dress it himself?'

'I bound my handkerchief on it,' replied the Girl. Her voice was low, almost a whisper.

'Where was the wound?'

'In the right shoulder,' she replied.

'Back or front?' insisted the scientist.

'Back,' she replied. 'Very near the arm, an inch or so below the level of the shoulder.'

Except for The Thinking Machine himself Hatch was the only person in the room to whom this statement meant anything, and he restrained a shout with difficulty.

'Now, Mr Mallory,' the scientist went on calmly, 'do you happen to know Dr Clarence Walpole?'

'I know of him, yes,' replied the detective. 'He is a man of considerable reputation.'

'Would you believe him under oath?'

'Why, certainly, of course.'

The Supreme Intelligence tugged at his bristly moustache.

'If Doctor Walpole should dress a wound and should later, under oath, point out its exact location, you would believe him?'

'Why, I'd have to, of course.'

'Very well,' commented The Thinking Machine tersely. 'Now I will state an incontrovertible scientific fact for your further enlightenment. You may verify it any way you choose. This is, briefly, that the blood corpuscles in man average 133 hundredths of an inch in diameter. Remember that, please: 133 hundredths of an inch. The system of measurement has reached a state of perfection almost incomprehensible to the man who does not understand.'

He paused for so long that Detective Mallory began to wriggle again. The others were leaning forward, listening with widely varied expressions on their faces.

'Now, Mr Mallory,' continued The Thinking Machine at last, 'one of your men shot twice at the Burglar in the automobile, as I understand it?'

'Yes – two shots.'

'Mr Cunningham?'

'Yes, Detective Cunningham.'

'Is he here now?'

The detective pressed a button on his desk and a uniformed man appeared. Instructions were given, and a moment later Detective Cunningham stood before them wonderingly.

'I suppose you can prove beyond any shadow of a doubt,' resumed the scientist, still addressing Mr Mallory, 'that two shots – and only two – were fired?'

'I can prove it by twenty witnesses,' was the reply.

'Good, very good,' exclaimed the scientist, and he turned to Cunningham. 'You know that only two shots were fired?'

'I know it, yes,' replied Cunningham. 'I fired 'em.'

'May I see your revolver?'

Cunningham produced the weapon and handed it over. The Thinking Machine merely glanced at it.

'This is the revolver you used?'

'Yes.'

'Very well, then,' remarked the scientist quietly, 'on that statement alone Mr Herbert is proven innocent of the charge against him.'

There was an astonished gasp all around. Hatch was beginning to see what The Thinking Machine meant, and curiously watched the bewitchingly sorrowful face of Dollie Meredith. He saw all sorts of strange things there.

'Proven innocent?' snorted Detective Mallory. 'Why, you've convicted him out of hand so far as I can see.'

'Corpuscles in human blood average, as I said, 133 hundredths of an inch in diameter,' resumed the scientist. 'They vary slightly each way, of course. Now, the corpuscles of the Burglar in the automobile measured just 131.47 hundredths of an inch. Mr Herbert's corpuscles, tested the same way, with the same instruments, measure precisely 135.60 hundredths.' He stopped as if that were all.

'By George!' exclaimed Mr Randolph. 'By George!'

'That's all tommy-rot,' Detective Mallory burst out. 'That's nothing to a jury or to any other man with common sense.'

'That difference in measurement proves beyond question that Mr Herbert was not wounded while in the automobile,' went on The Thinking Machine as if there had been no interruption. 'Now, Mr Cunningham, may I ask if the Burglar's back was toward you when you fired?'

'Yes, I suppose so. He was going away from me.'

'Well, that statement agrees with the statement of Miss Meredith to show that the Burglar was wounded in the back. Doctor Walpole dressed Mr Herbert's wound between two and three o'clock Friday morning following the masked ball. Mr Herbert had been shot, but the wound was in the front of his right shoulder.'

Delighted amazement radiated from Dollie Meredith's face; she clapped her hands involuntarily as she would have applauded a stage incident. Detective Mallory started to say something, then thought better of it and glared at Cunningham instead.

'Now, Mr Cunningham says that he shot the Burglar with this revolver.' The Thinking Machine waved the weapon under Detective Mallory's nose. 'This is the usual police weapon. Its calibre is thirty-eight. Mr Herbert was shot with a thirty-two calibre. Here is the bullet.' And he tossed it on the desk.

CHAPTER 6

Strange emotions all tangled up with turbulent, nightmarish impressions scrambled through Dollie Meredith's pretty head in garish disorder. She didn't know whether to laugh or cry. Finally she compromised by blushing radiantly at the memory of certain lingering kisses she had bestowed upon – upon – Dick Herbert? No, it wasn't Dick Herbert. Oh, dear!

Detective Mallory pounced upon the bullet as a hound upon a hare, and turned and twisted it in his hands. Cunningham leaned over his shoulder, then drew a cartridge from the revolver and compared it, as to size, with the bullet. Hatch and Mr Randolph, looking on, saw him shake his head. The ball was too small for the revolver.

The Supreme Intelligence turned suddenly, fiercely, upon Dollie and thrust an accusing finger into her startled face.

'Mr Herbert confessed to you that he was with you in the automobile, didn't he?'

'Y-yes,' she faltered.

'You know he was with you?'

'I thought I knew it.'

'You wouldn't have gone with any other man?'

'Certainly not!' A blaze of indignation suffused her cheeks.

'Your casket of jewels was found among the stolen goods in his possession?'

'Yes, but –'

With a wave of his hand the Supreme Intelligence stopped explanations and turned to glare at The Thinking Machine. That imperturbable gentleman did not alter his position in the slightest, nor did he change the steady, upward squint of his eyes.

'If you have quite finished, Mr Mallory,' he said after a moment, 'I will explain how and in what circumstances the stolen plate and jewels came into Mr Herbert's possession.'

'Go on,' urged Mr Randolph and Hatch in a breath.

'Explain all you please; I've got him with the goods on him,' declared the Supreme Intelligence doggedly.

'When the simplest rules of logic establish a fact it becomes incontrovertible,' resumed the scientist. 'I have shown that Mr Herbert was not the man in the automobile – the Burglar. Now, what did happen to Mr Herbert? Twice since his arrest he has stated that it would be useless for him to explain because no one would believe it, and no one would have believed it unsupported, least of all you, Mr Mallory.

'It's an admitted fact that Miss Meredith and Mr Herbert had planned to elope from Seven Oaks the night of the ball. I daresay that Mr Herbert did not deem it wise for Miss Meredith to know his costume, although he must, of necessity, have known hers. Therefore, the plan was for him to recognise her, but as it developed she recognised him – or thought she did – and that was the real cause of this remarkable muddle.' He glanced at Dollie. 'Is that correct?'

Dollie nodded blushingly.

'Now, Mr Herbert did not go to the ball – why not I will explain later. Therefore, Miss Meredith recognised the real Burglar as Mr Herbert, and we know how they ran away together after the Burglar had stolen the plate and various articles of jewelry. We must credit the Burglar with remarkable intelligence, so that when a young and attractive woman – I may say a beautiful woman – spoke to him as someone else he immediately saw an advantage in it. For instance, when there came discovery of the theft the girl might unwittingly throw the police off the track by revealing to them what she

117

believed to be the identity of the thief. Further, he was a daring, audacious sort of person; the pure love of such an adventure might have appealed to him. Still, again, it is possible that he believed Miss Meredith a thief who was in peril of discovery or capture, and a natural gallantry for one of his own craft prompted him to act as he did. There is always, too, the possibility that he knew he was mistaken for Mr Herbert.'

Dollie was beginning to see, too.

'We know the method of escape, the pursuit, and all that,' continued the Professor, 'therefore we jump to the return of the gold plate. Logic makes it instantly apparent that that was the work of Miss Meredith here. Not having the plate, Mr Herbert did not send it back, of course; and the Burglar would not have sent it back. Realising, too late, that the man she was with was really a thief – and still believing him, perhaps, to be Mr Herbert – she must have taken the plate and escaped under cover of darkness?'

The tone carried a question and The Thinking Machine turned squintingly upon Dollie. Again she nodded. She was enthralled, fascinated, by the recital.

'It was a simple matter for her to return the gold plate by express, taking advantage of an unoccupied house and the willingness of a stranger to telephone for an express wagon. Thus, we have the plate again at Seven Oaks, and we have it there by the only method it could have been returned there when we account for, and consider, every known fact.'

The Thinking Machine paused and sat silently staring upward. His listeners readjusted themselves in their chairs and waited impatiently.

'Now, why did Mr Herbert confess to Miss Meredith that he stole the plate?' asked the scientist, as if of himself. 'Perhaps she forced him to it. Mr Herbert is a young man of strong loyalty and a grim sense of humour, this latter being a quality the police are not acquainted with. However, Mr Herbert did confess to Miss Meredith that he was the Burglar, but he made this confession, obviously, because she would believe nothing else, and when a seeming necessity of protecting the real Burglar was still uppermost in his mind. What he wanted was the Girl. If the facts never came out he was all right; if they did come out they would implicate one whom he was protecting, but through no fault of his – therefore, he was still all right.'

'Bah!' exclaimed the Supreme Intelligence. 'My experience has shown that a man doesn't confess to a theft unless –'

'So we may safely assume,' The Thinking Machine continued almost pleasantly, 'that Mr Herbert, by confessing the theft as a prank, perhaps, won back Miss Meredith's confidence; that they planned an elopement for the second time. A conversation Mr Hatch had with Mr Herbert immediately after Mr Herbert saw Miss Meredith practically confirms it. Then, with matters in this shape, the real Burglar, to whom I have accredited unusual powers, stole the plate the second time – we know how.'

'Herbert stole it, you mean!' blazed Detective Mallory.

'This theft came immediately on top of the reconciliation of Miss Meredith and Mr Herbert,' The Thinking Machine went on steadily, without heeding the remark by the slightest sign. 'Therefore, it was only natural that he should be the person most vitally interested in seeing that the plate was again returned. He undertook to do this himself. The result was that, where the police had failed, he found the plate and a lot of jewels, took them from the Burglar, and was about to return Mr Randolph's property when the detectives walked in on him. That is why he laughed.'

Detective Mallory arose from his seat and started to say something impolite. The presence of Dollie Meredith choked the words back and he swallowed hard.

'Who then,' he demanded after a couple of gulps – 'who do you say is the thief if Herbert is not?'

The Thinking Machine glanced up into his face, then turned to Hatch.

'Mr Hatch, what is that name I asked you to get?'

'George Francis Hayden,' was the stammering reply, 'but – but –'

'Then George Francis Hayden is the thief,' declared The Thinking Machine emphatically.

'But I – I started to say,' Hatch blurted – 'I started to say that George Francis Hayden has been dead for two years.'

The Thinking Machine rose suddenly and glared at the reporter. There was a tense silence, broken at last by a chuckle from Detective Mallory.

'Dead?' repeated the scientist incredulously. 'Do you know that?'

'Yes, I – I know it.'

The Thinking Machine stood for another moment squinting at him, then, turning, left the room.

CHAPTER 7

Half an hour later The Thinking Machine walked in, un-announced, upon Dick Herbert. The front door had not been locked; Blair was somewhere in the rear. Herbert, in some surprise, glanced up at his visitor just in time to see him plonk himself down solidly into a chair.

'Mr Herbert,' the scientist began, 'I have gone out of my way to prove to the police that you were not in the automobile with Miss Meredith, and that you did not steal the gold plate found in your possession. Now, I happen to know the name of the thief, and –'

'And if you mention it to one living soul,' Dick added suddenly, hotly, 'I shall forget myself and – and –'

'His name is George Francis Hayden,' the scientist continued.

Dick started a little and straightened up; the menace dropped from him and he paused to gaze curiously into the wizened face before him. After a moment he drew a sigh of deep relief.

'Oh!' he exclaimed. 'Oh!'

'I know that that isn't who you thought it was,' resumed the other, 'but the fact remains that Hayden is the man with whom Miss Meredith unwittingly eloped, and that Hayden is the man who actually stole the plate and jewels. Further, the fact remains that Hayden –'

'Is dead,' Dick supplemented grimly. 'You are talking through your –' He coughed a little. 'You are talking without any knowledge of what you are saying.'

'He can't be dead,' remarked the scientist calmly.

'But he is dead!' Dick insisted.

'He can't be dead,' snapped the other abruptly. 'It's perfectly silly to suppose such a thing. Why, I have proven absolutely, by the simplest rules of logic, that he stole the gold plate, therefore he cannot be dead. It's silly to say so.'

Dick wasn't quite certain whether to be angry or amused. He decided to hold the matter in abeyance for the moment and see what other strange thing would develop.

'How long has he been dead?' continued the scientist.

'About two years.'

'You know it?'

'Yes, I know it.'

'How do you know it?'

'Because I attended his funeral,' was the prompt reply. Dick saw a shadow of impatience flash into his visitor's face and instantly pass.

'How did he die?' queried the scientist.

'He was lost from his catboat,' Dick answered. 'He had gone out sailing, alone, while in a bathing-suit. Several hours after the boat drifted in on the tide without him. Two or three weeks later the body was recovered.'

'Ah!' exclaimed The Thinking Machine.

Then, for half an hour or so, he talked, and – as he went on, incisively, pointedly, dramatically, even, at times – Dick Herbert's eyes opened wider and wider. At the end he rose and gripped the scientist's slender white fingers heartily in his own with something approaching awe in his manner. Finally he put on his hat and they went out together.

That evening at eight o'clock Detective Mallory, Hutchinson Hatch, Mr Randolph, Mr Meredith, Mr Greyton, and Dollie Meredith gathered in a parlour of the Greyton home by request of The Thinking Machine. They were waiting for something – no one knew exactly what.

Finally there came a tinkle at the bell and The Thinking Machine entered. Behind him came Dick Herbert, Dr

Clarence Walpole, and a stranger. Mr Meredith glanced up quickly at Herbert, and Dollie lifted her chin haughtily with a stony stare which admitted of no compromise. Dick pleaded for recognition with his eyes, but it was no use, so he sat down where he could watch her unobserved.

Singular expressions flitted over the countenance of the Supreme Intelligence. Right here, now, he knew the earth was to be jerked out from under him and he was not at all certain that there would be anything left for him to cling to. This first impression was strengthened when The Thinking Machine introduced Doctor Walpole with an ostentatious squint at Mr Mallory. The detective set his teeth hard.

The Thinking Machine sat down, stretched out his slender legs, turned his eyes upward, and adjusted his fingers precisely, tip to tip. The others watched him anxiously.

'We will have to go back a few years to get the real beginning of the events which have culminated so strangely within the past week,' he said. 'This was a close friendship of three young men in college. They were Mr Herbert here, a freshman, and Harry Meredith and George Francis Hayden, juniors. This friendship, not an unusual one in college, was made somewhat romantic by the young men styling themselves The Triangle. They occupied the same apartments and were exclusive to a degree. Of necessity Mr Herbert was drawn from that exclusiveness, to a certain extent by his participation in football.'

A germ of memory was working in Hatch's mind.

'At someone's suggestion three triangular watch charms were made, identical in every way save for initials on the back. They bore a symbol which was meaningless except to The Triangle. They were made to order and are, therefore, the only three of the kind in the world. Mr Herbert has one now on his watch chain, with his own initials; there is another with the initials 'G.F.H.' in the lot of jewelry Mr Mallory recovered from Mr Herbert. The third is worn by Harry Meredith, who is now in Buenos Aires. The American Consul there has confirmed, by cable, that fact.

'In the senior year the three young men of The Triangle were concerned in the mysterious disappearance of a valuable diamond ring. It was hushed up in college after it seemed established that Mr Herbert was a thief. Knowing his own innocence and seeing what seemed to be an exclusive opportunity for Harry Meredith to have done what was charged, Mr Herbert laid the matter to him, having at that time an interview with Harry's father. The result of that interview was more than ever to convince Mr Meredith of Mr Herbert's guilt. As a matter of fact, the thief in that case was George Francis Hayden.'

There were little murmurs of astonishment, and Mr Meredith turned and stared at Dick Herbert. Dollie gave him a little glance out of a corner of her eye, smiled, then sat up primly.

'This ended The Triangle,' resumed the scientist. 'A year or so later Mr Herbert met Miss Meredith. About two years ago George Francis Hayden was reported drowned from his catboat. This was confirmed, apparently, by the finding of his body, and an insurance company paid over a large sum – I think it was $25,000 – to a woman who said she was his wife. But George Francis Hayden was not drowned; he is alive now. It was a carefully planned fraud against the insurance company, and it succeeded.

'This, then, was the situation on last Thursday – the night of the masked ball at Seven Oaks – except that there had grown up a love affair between Miss Meredith and Mr Herbert. Naturally, the father opposed this because of the incident in college. Both Miss Meredith and Mr Herbert had invitations to that ball. It was an opportunity for an elopement and they accepted it. Mr Herbert sent word to her what costume to wear; she did not know the nature of his.

'On Thursday afternoon Miss Meredith sent her jewel-casket, with practically all her jewels, to Mr Herbert. She wanted them, naturally; they probably planned a trip abroad. The maid in this house took the casket and gave it into Mr Herbert's own hands. Am I right?' He turned squarely and squinted at Dollie.

'Yes,' she gasped quickly. She smiled distractingly upon her father and he made some violent remarks to himself.

'At this point, Fate, in the guise of a masked Burglar, saw fit to step into the affair,' the scientist went on after a moment. 'About nine-thirty, Thursday evening, while Mr Herbert was alone, the masked Burglar, George Francis Hayden, entered Mr Herbert's house, possibly thinking everyone was away. There, still masked, he met Mr Herbert, who – by something the Burglar said and by the triangular charm he wore – recognised him as Harry Meredith. Remember, he thought he knew George Francis Hayden was dead.

'There were some words and a personal encounter between the two men. George Francis Hayden fired a shot which struck Mr Herbert in the right shoulder – in front – took the jewel-casket in which Mr Herbert had placed his card of invitation to the ball, and went away, leaving Mr Herbert senseless on the floor.'

Dollie's face blanched suddenly and she gasped. When she glanced involuntarily at Dick she read the love-light in his eyes, and her colour returned with a rush.

'Several hours later, when Mr Herbert recovered consciousness,' the unruffled voice went on, 'he went to Doctor

Walpole, the nearest physician, and there the bullet was extracted and the wound dressed. The ball was thirty-two calibre?'

Doctor Walpole nodded.

'And Mr Cunningham's revolver carried a thirty-eight,' added the scientist. 'Now we go back to the Burglar. He found the invitation in the casket, and the bold scheme, which later he carried out so perfectly, came to him as an inspiration. He went to the ball just as he was. Nerve, self-possession, and humour took him through. We know the rest of that.

'Naturally, in the circumstances, Mr Herbert, believing that Harry Meredith was the thief, would say nothing to bring disgrace upon the name of the girl he loved. Instead, he saw Miss Meredith, who would not accept his denial then, and in order to get her first – explanations might come later – he confessed to the theft, whereupon they planned the second elopement.

'When Miss Meredith returned the plate by express there was no anticipation of a second theft. Here is where we get a better understanding of the mettle of the real Burglar – George Francis Hayden. He went back and got the plate from Seven Oaks. Instantly that upset the second elopement plan. Then Mr Herbert undertook the search, got a clue, followed it, and recovered not only the plate, but a great lot of jewels.'

There was a pause. A skyrocket ascended in Hatch's mind and burst, illuminating the whole tangled story. Detective Mallory sat dumbly, thinking harsh words. Mr Meredith arose, went over to Dick Herbert, and solemnly shook his hand, after which he sat down again. Dollie smiled charmingly.

'Now that is what actually happened,' said The Thinking Machine, after a little while. 'How do I know it? Logic, logic, logic! The logical mind can start from any given point and go backward or forward, with equal facility, to a natural conclusion. This is as certain as that two and two make four – not sometimes, but all the time.

'First in this case I had Mr Hatch's detailed examination of each circumstance. By an inspiration he connected Mr Herbert and Miss Meredith with the affair and talked to both before the police had any knowledge at all of them. In other words, he reached at a bound what they took days to accomplish. After the second theft he came to me and related the story.'

The reporter blushed modestly.

'Mr Hatch's belief that the things that had happened to Mr Herbert and Miss Meredith bore on the theft,' resumed the scientist, 'was susceptible of confirmation or refutation in only one way, this being so because of Mr Herbert's silence – due to his loyalty. I saw that. But, before I went further, I saw clearly what had actually happened if I presupposed that there had been some connection. Thus came to me, I may say here, the almost certain knowledge that Miss Meredith had a brother, although I had never heard of him or her.'

He paused a little and twiddled his thumbs thoughtfully.

'Suppose you give us just your line of reasoning,' ventured Hatch.

'Well, I began with the bloodstains in the automobile to either bring Mr Herbert into this affair or shut him out,' replied the scientist. 'You know how I made the blood tests. They showed conclusively that the blood on the cushion was not Mr Herbert's. Remember, please, that, although I knew Miss Meredith had been in the automobile, I also knew she was not wounded; therefore the blood was that of someone else – the man.

'Now, I knew Mr Herbert had been wounded – he wouldn't say how. If at home, would he not go to the nearest physician? Probably. I got Doctor Walpole's name from the telephone-book – he being nearest the Herbert home – and sent Mr Hatch there, where he learned of the wound in front, and of the thirty-two calibre ball. I already knew the police revolvers were thirty-eight calibre; therefore Mr Herbert was not wounded while in the automobile.

'That removed Mr Herbert as a possibility in the first theft, despite the fact that his invitation-card was presented at the door. It was reasonable to suppose that invitation had been stolen. Immediately after the plate was returned by express, Mr Herbert effected a reconciliation with Miss Meredith. Because of this and for other reasons I could not bring myself to see that he was a party to the second theft, as I knew him to be innocent of the first. Yet, what happened to him? Why wouldn't he say something?

'All things must be imagined before they can be achieved; therefore imagination is one of the most vital parts of the scientific brain. In this instance I could only imagine why Mr Herbert was silent. Remember, he was shot and wouldn't say who did it. Why? If it had been an ordinary thief – and I got the idea of a thief from the invitation-card being in other hands than his – he would not have hesitated to talk. Therefore, it was an extraordinary thief in that it connected with something near and dear to him. No one was nearer and dearer to him than Miss Meredith. Did she shoot him? No. Did her father shoot him? Probably not, but possibly. A brother? That began to look more reasonable. Mr Herbert would probably not have gone so far to protect one less near to her than brother or father.

'For the moment I assumed a brother, not knowing. How did Mr Herbert know this brother? Was it in his college days? Mr Hatch brought me a list of the students of three years before his graduating year and there I found the name, Harry Meredith. You see, step by step, pure logic was leading me to something tangible, definite. My next act was to see Mr Meredith and ask for the address of his son – an only son – whom at that time I frankly believed was the real thief. But this son was in South America. That startled me a little and brought me up against the father as a possible thief. He was in Baltimore on that night.

'I accepted that as true at the moment after some – er – some pleasant words with Mr Meredith. Then the question: was the man who stole from Mr Herbert, probably entering his place and shooting him, masked? Mr Herbert said he was. I framed the question so as to bring Harry Meredith's name into it, much to Mr Herbert's alarm. How had he recognised him as Harry Meredith? By something he said or wore? Mr Herbert replied in the affirmative – both. Therefore I had a masked Burglar who could not have been either Harry Meredith or Harry Meredith's father. Who was he?

'I decided to let Mr Hatch look into that point for me, and went to see Doctor Walpole. He gave me the bullet he had extracted from Mr Herbert's shoulder. Mr Hatch, shortly after, rushed in on me with the statement that Miss Meredith had admitted that Mr Herbert had confessed to her. I could see instantly why he had confessed to her. Then Mr Hatch undertook for me the investigation of Herbert's and Harry Meredith's careers in college. He remembered part of it and unearthed the affair of The Triangle and the theft of a diamond ring.

'I had asked Mr Hatch to find for me if Harry Meredith and Mr Herbert had had a mutual intimate in college. They had: George Francis Hayden, the third member of the Triangle. Then the question seemed to be solved, but Mr Hatch upset everything when he said that Mr Hayden was dead. I went immediately to see Mr Herbert. From him I learned that, although Mr Hayden was supposed to be dead and buried, there was no positive proof of it; the body recovered had been in the water three weeks and was consequently almost unrecognisable. Therefore, the theft came inevitably to Mr Hayden. Why? Because the Burglar had been recognised by something he said and wore. It would have been difficult for Mr Herbert to recognise a masked man so positively unless the masked man wore something he absolutely knew, or said something he absolutely knew. Mr Herbert thought with reason that the masked man was Harry Meredith, but, with Harry Meredith in South America, the thief was incontrovertibly George Francis Hayden. There was no going behind that.

'After a short interview as to Hayden, during which Mr Herbert told me more of The Triangle and the three watch charms, he and I went out investigating. He took me to the room where he had found the plate and jewels – a place in an apartment-house which this gentleman manages.' The scientist turned to the stranger, who had been a silent listener. 'He identified an old photograph of George Francis Hayden as an occupant of an apartment.

'Mr Herbert and I searched the place. My growing idea, based on the established knavery of George Francis Hayden, that he was the real thief in the college incident, was proven when I found this ring there – the ring that was stolen at that time – with the initials of the owner in it.'

The Thinking Machine produced the ring and offered it to Detective Mallory, who had allowed the earth to slip away from him slowly but surely, and he examined it with a new and absorbed interest.

'Mr Herbert and I learned of the insurance fraud in another manner – that is, when we knew that George Francis Hayden was not dead, we knew there had been a fraud. Mr Hayden has been known lately as Chester Goodrich. He has been missing since Mr Herbert, in his absence, recovered the plate and the jewels in his apartments. I may add that, up to the day of the masked ball, he was protected from casual recognition by a full beard. He is now clean-shaven.'

The Thinking Machine glanced at Mr Mallory.

'Your man – Downey, I think it was – did excellent work,' he said, 'in tracing Miss Meredith from the time she left the automobile until she returned home, and later leading you to Mr Herbert. It was not strange that you should have been convinced of his guilt when we consider the goods found in his possession and also the wound in his shoulder. The only trouble is he didn't get to the real insides of it.'

That was all. For a long time there was silence. Dollie Meredith's pretty face was radiant and her eyes were fastened on her father. Mr Meredith glanced at her, cleared his throat several times, then arose and offered his hand to Dick Herbert.

'I have done you an injustice, sir,' he said gravely. 'Permit me to apologise. I think perhaps my daughter –'

That was superfluous. Dollie was already beside Dick, and a rousing, smacking, resounding kiss echoed her father's words. Dick liked it some and was ready for more, but Dollie impetuously flung her arms around the neck of The Thinking Machine, and he – passed to his reward.

'You dear old thing!' she gurgled. 'You're just too sweet and cute for anything.'

'Dear me! Dear me!' fussed The Thinking Machine. 'Don't do that. It annoys me exceedingly.'

Some three months later, when the search for George Francis Hayden had become only lukewarm, this being three days before Miss Meredith's wedding to Dick Herbert, she received a small box containing a solitaire ring and a note. It was brief:

> In memory of one night in the woods and of what happened there, permit me to give this – you can't return it. It is one of the few things honest money from me ever paid for.
>
> Bill, the Burglar.

While Dollie examined the ring with mingled emotions Dick stared at the postmark on the package.

'It's a corking good clue,' he said enthusiastically.

Dollie turned to him, recognising a menace in the words, and took the paper which bore the postmark from his hands.

'Let's pretend,' she said gently – 'let's pretend we don't know where it came from!'

Dick stared a little and kissed her.

Jacques Futrelle was born in 1875. Beginning his career as a journalist at the age of eighteen, he worked for a number of newspapers, including *the New York Herald* and *The Boston Post*. His career as detective writer began with *The Problem of Cell 13* which was serialised in *The Boston American* in 1905, featuring for the first time 'The Thinking Machine', the character which was to prove his most prolific, Professor S.F.X. Van Dusen. He would later forge a career as a highly productive author of novels, becoming well-known and respected. His most famous works include *The Thinking Machine*, *The Diamond Master* and *The High Hand*.

In 1895 he married Lily Peel and they went on to have two children. His literary career was interspersed with stints as a playwright and actor in Richmond, Virginia.

Following a trip to Europe in 1912, Futrelle died aboard the Titanic, having safely ensured that his wife had been placed aboard a lifeboat. Futrelle's last work, *My Lady's Garter*, was published posthumously later in 1912 and was inscribed with a note from Lily: 'To the heroes of the Titanic, I dedicate this my husband's book.'

HESPERUS PRESS

Hesperus Press is committed to bringing near what is far – far both in space and time. Works written by the greatest authors, and unjustly neglected or simply little known in the English-speaking world, are made accessible through new translations and a completely fresh editorial approach. Through these classic works, the reader is introduced to the greatest writers from all times and all cultures.

For more information on Hesperus Press, please visit our website: **www.hesperuspress.com**

SELECTED TITLES FROM HESPERUS PRESS

Author	Title	Foreword writer
Pietro Aretino	*The School of Whoredom*	Paul Bailey
Pietro Aretino	*The Secret Life of Nuns*	
Jane Austen	*Lesley Castle*	Zoë Heller
Jane Austen	*Love and Friendship*	Fay Weldon
Honoré de Balzac	*Colonel Chabert*	A.N. Wilson
Charles Baudelaire	*On Wine and Hashish*	Margaret Drabble
Giovanni Boccaccio	*Life of Dante*	A.N. Wilson
Charlotte Brontë	*The Spell*	
Emily Brontë	*Poems of Solitude*	Helen Dunmore
Mikhail Bulgakov	*Fatal Eggs*	Doris Lessing
Mikhail Bulgakov	*The Heart of a Dog*	A.S. Byatt
Giacomo Casanova	*The Duel*	Tim Parks
Miguel de Cervantes	*The Dialogue of the Dogs*	Ben Okri
Geoffrey Chaucer	*The Parliament of Birds*	
Anton Chekhov	*The Story of a Nobody*	Louis de Bernières
Anton Chekhov	*Three Years*	William Fiennes
Wilkie Collins	*The Frozen Deep*	
Joseph Conrad	*Heart of Darkness*	A.N. Wilson
Joseph Conrad	*The Return*	Colm Tóibín
Gabriele D'Annunzio	*The Book of the Virgins*	Tim Parks
Dante Alighieri	*The Divine Comedy: Inferno*	
Dante Alighieri	*New Life*	Louis de Bernières
Daniel Defoe	*The King of Pirates*	Peter Ackroyd
Marquis de Sade	*Incest*	Janet Street-Porter
Charles Dickens	*The Haunted House*	Peter Ackroyd
Charles Dickens	*A House to Let*	
Fyodor Dostoevsky	*The Double*	Jeremy Dyson
Fyodor Dostoevsky	*Poor People*	Charlotte Hobson
Alexandre Dumas	*One Thousand and One Ghosts*	

George Eliot	*Amos Barton*	Matthew Sweet
Henry Fielding	*Jonathan Wild the Great*	Peter Ackroyd
F. Scott Fitzgerald	*The Popular Girl*	Helen Dunmore
Gustave Flaubert	*Memoirs of a Madman*	Germaine Greer
Ugo Foscolo	*Last Letters of Jacopo Ortis*	Valerio Massimo Manfredi
Elizabeth Gaskell	*Lois the Witch*	Jenny Uglow
Théophile Gautier	*The Jinx*	Gilbert Adair
André Gide	*Theseus*	
Johann Wolfgang von Goethe	*The Man of Fifty*	A.S. Byatt
Nikolai Gogol	*The Squabble*	Patrick McCabe
E.T.A. Hoffmann	*Mademoiselle de Scudéri*	Gilbert Adair
Victor Hugo	*The Last Day of a Condemned Man*	Libby Purves
Joris-Karl Huysmans	*With the Flow*	Simon Callow
Henry James	*In the Cage*	Libby Purves
Franz Kafka	*Metamorphosis*	Martin Jarvis
Franz Kafka	*The Trial*	Zadie Smith
John Keats	*Fugitive Poems*	Andrew Motion
Heinrich von Kleist	*The Marquise of O–*	Andrew Miller
Mikhail Lermontov	*A Hero of Our Time*	Doris Lessing
Nikolai Leskov	*Lady Macbeth of Mtsensk*	Gilbert Adair
Carlo Levi	*Words are Stones*	Anita Desai
Xavier de Maistre	*A Journey Around my Room*	Alain de Botton
André Malraux	*The Way of the Kings*	Rachel Seiffert
Katherine Mansfield	*Prelude*	William Boyd
Edgar Lee Masters	*Spoon River Anthology*	Shena Mackay
Guy de Maupassant	*Butterball*	Germaine Greer
Prosper Mérimée	*Carmen*	Philip Pullman
Sir Thomas More	*The History of King Richard III*	Sister Wendy Beckett
Sándor Petőfi	*John the Valiant*	George Szirtes

Francis Petrarch	*My Secret Book*	Germaine Greer
Luigi Pirandello	*Loveless Love*	
Edgar Allan Poe	*Eureka*	Sir Patrick Moore
Alexander Pope	*The Rape of the Lock and A Key to the Lock*	Peter Ackroyd
Antoine-François Prévost	*Manon Lescaut*	Germaine Greer
Marcel Proust	*Pleasures and Days*	A.N. Wilson
Alexander Pushkin	*Dubrovsky*	Patrick Neate
Alexander Pushkin	*Ruslan and Lyudmila*	Colm Tóibín
François Rabelais	*Pantagruel*	Paul Bailey
François Rabelais	*Gargantua*	Paul Bailey
Christina Rossetti	*Commonplace*	Andrew Motion
George Sand	*The Devil's Pool*	Victoria Glendinning
Jean-Paul Sartre	*The Wall*	Justin Cartwright
Friedrich von Schiller	*The Ghost-seer*	Martin Jarvis
Mary Shelley	*Transformation*	
Percy Bysshe Shelley	*Zastrozzi*	Germaine Greer
Stendhal	*Memoirs of an Egotist*	Doris Lessing
Robert Louis Stevenson	*Dr Jekyll and Mr Hyde*	Helen Dunmore
Theodor Storm	*The Lake of the Bees*	Alan Sillitoe
Leo Tolstoy	*The Death of Ivan Ilych*	
Leo Tolstoy	*Hadji Murat*	Colm Tóibín
Ivan Turgenev	*Faust*	Simon Callow
Mark Twain	*The Diary of Adam and Eve*	John Updike
Mark Twain	*Tom Sawyer, Detective*	
Oscar Wilde	*The Portrait of Mr W.H.*	Peter Ackroyd
Virginia Woolf	*Carlyle's House and Other Sketches*	Doris Lessing
Virginia Woolf	*Monday or Tuesday*	Scarlett Thomas
Emile Zola	*For a Night of Love*	A.N. Wilson